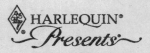

HARLEQUIN®
Presents

What do you love most about reading
Harlequin Presents books? From what you
tell us, it's our sexy foreign heroes, exciting
and emotionally intense relationships,
generous helpings of pure passion and
glamorous international settings that bring
you pleasure!

Welcome to February 2007's stunning
selection of eight novels that bring you
emotion, passion and excitement galore,
as you are whisked around the world to meet
men who make love in many languages. And
you'll also find your favorite authors:
Penny Jordan, Lucy Monroe, Kate Walker,
Susan Stephens, Sandra Field, Carole Mortimer,
Elizabeth Power and Anne McAllister.

Sit back and let us entertain you....

Spent at the sheikh's pleasure…

by
Penny Jordan

The Sheikh's Virgin Bride
One Night with the Sheikh
Possessed by the Sheikh
Prince of the Desert
Taken by the Sheikh

Welcome to the exotic lands of Zuran,
and Dhurahn, beautiful, sand-swept places
where sheikhs rule and anything is possible…

Experience nights of passion
under a desert moon!

Available only from Harlequin Presents®

Penny Jordan

TAKEN BY
THE SHEIKH

Arabian Nights

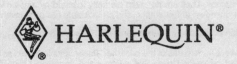

HARLEQUIN®

TORONTO • NEW YORK • LONDON
AMSTERDAM • PARIS • SYDNEY • HAMBURG
STOCKHOLM • ATHENS • TOKYO • MILAN • MADRID
PRAGUE • WARSAW • BUDAPEST • AUCKLAND

ISBN-13: 978-0-373-23367-0
ISBN-10:   0-373-23367-1

TAKEN BY THE SHEIKH

First North American Publication 2007.

www.eHarlequin.com

Printed in U.S.A.

PROLOGUE

'SO THE negotiations went well, then?'

Drax frowned, his dark, arrogantly slanted eyebrows snapping together over an equally arrogant aquiline nose. Although his brother had welcomed him back to the small Arab emirate they ruled together with his usual warmth, Drax sensed that there was something on his elder twin's mind that Vere had not yet revealed to him.

'The talks in London went very well,' he confirmed. He and Vere had ruled Dhurahn together now for almost a full decade, having come to power just after their twenty-fifth birthday, following the death of their parents in a car accident during a state visit.

Despite their closeness, they had never talked about the horror of that time—or the loss of their strong, energetic and forward-thinking father and their beautiful Irish mother. There had been no need. As twins they instinctively understood each other's feelings. Physically they were identical, but when it came to their personalities sometimes it seemed to Drax that they were two halves of one whole—sharing the same basic mind-set and understanding, and yet manifesting a desire to follow their shared life path in different ways.

Drax had come straight to his brother's private audience room from the airport without bothering to go to his own quarters first to change. So, while Vere was dressed traditionally in a robe of dark blue embroidered with gold, worn over his white dishdasha, his head covered, Drax was wearing a formal dark blue business suit, the jacket open over a crisp white shirt worn with a discreetly striped dark red silk tie.

However, although their mode of dress could not have been more different, that faded into insignificance against the impact of their identical and magnificent physical appearance.

They were both tall and broad-shouldered, with the same slightly hooded ice-green eyes which could glitter with fierce heat, and the same distinctive predatory profiles. Their Berber blood, mixed with French and then Irish, had ensured they possessed an aura of power and sexuality that went beyond easy good looks to something that would have been dark and dangerous enough in one man, but when doubled possessed a force that was un-nerving and compelling.

'We both know that we aren't the only Middle Eastern country wanting to establish ourselves as not just the Arab world's recog-nised premier financial centre but the one with the strongest links to the recognised financial centres throughout the world. However, from the talks I had in London I gained the impres-sion that we are the favoured choice. As we agreed, I made it clear that Dhurahn is prepared to put aside an enclave of one hundred acres of land to house the buildings needed to develop and grow a "knowledge economy", and that we favour the use of English mercantile law because of its princi-ples of equity and fairness. I also told them we envisage developing a financial exchange that will equal anything that New York, Hong Kong or London has to offer, with a regulatory system that investors and the business community can rely on and trust. But that's enough about what I've been doing in London, Vere. Something's on your mind.'

Vere raised one eyebrow in silent recognition of his twin's astuteness.

'Yes,' he admitted. 'We have a problem.'

Drax looked searchingly at his twin. 'And that problem is?'

'While you were in London we were contacted by both the Ruler of Zuran and the Emir of Khulua.'

Drax waited. There was nothing particularly unusual in them being contacted by their closest neighbours; they were on good terms. Dhurahn did not have the large oil reserves and revenues enjoyed by its neighbours, but its long river made the land rich and fertile, and Dhurahn had become the 'greenhouse' that supplied Zuran, in particular, with fresh produce for its expanding tourist industry. The days when the fiercely warring tribes had fought bitterly over the hot desert sands were long gone, and the people of Dhurahn lived in peace with their neighbours, enjoying a mutual and shared prosperity.

But certain tribal methods of ensuring peace still endured.

'Both the Ruler and the Emir have, in the mysterious ways of such things—the desert wind is, as ever, capricious in where it blows—heard rumours of our plans,' Vere told his brother dryly. 'Not that they said as much, but of course it is obvious why they are both now so eager to cement the existing good relationship we share with them.'

'You are telling me this—but what is it that you are *not* telling me?' Drax demanded, easily recognising that his brother was withholding something. 'To keep on good terms with our neighbours makes sound business sense…'

'What the Ruler and the Emir are so keen to discuss with us is the matter of our marriages.'

'*Our* marriages?' Drax frowned again. They were thirty-four. One day, of course, they would both marry, choosing their wives carefully and with due consideration for the future of their country, but that time was not here yet. Right now they had far more important things to do—like establishing Dhurahn as the strongest financial powerhouse in the region.

'Our marriages,' Vere repeated grimly. 'Yours to the Emir's eldest daughter and mine to the Ruler's youngest sister.'

The two brothers looked at one another.

'Such marriages would strengthen our ties with both countries, but it would also strengthen *their* potential involvement with Dhurahn,' Drax pointed out. 'While we stand between them, and get on well with both the Ruler and the Emir, there are issues on which they do not agree. The Emir has never approved of the Ruler's decision to expand Zuran's involvement with the tourist industry. Currently we hold the balance of power between them, and ours is in many ways the stronger position.'

'And, while he is loath to admit it, the Emir is jealous of the growing financial status and success of Zuran, and eager to match it. If we agree to their suggestion and take as wives members of their families both of them will try to use the link marriage creates to demand greater allegiance and support from us: in effect to control the power we hold. We can't let that happen. Apart from anything else it could, theoretically, mean that there might come a time when our loyalty to one another and Dhurahn could be in conflict with the loyalty demanded of us by our wives and their families.'

'And if we don't agree we'll risk offending both the Ruler and the Emir, causing them to lose face, and we can't afford to be on bad terms. It could harm our plans to establish Dhurahn as the financial and business capital of the region.'

'Yes.'

Angrily Drax paced the floor. 'We cannot allow ourselves to be manipulated like this.'

'Neither of us wants to be tied via marriage to either of our neighbours,' Vere agreed grimly. 'Dhurahn must always govern its own future, and it is our duty to ensure that it does.'

'But, as you said, if we refuse then we risk offending two very powerful men.' Drax thought quickly. 'Unless, of course, we tell them that we are refusing because we are committed to marriage elsewhere. That way they'd stop pressuring us and they wouldn't lose face.'

'And when they discover that we are *not* getting married?'

'Do they need to discover that?' Drax asked. Vere was frowning but Drax persevered coolly. 'Both the Ruler and the Emir know that it is the tradition for our family and our people to take only one wife. It is not, surely, an insurmountable task to find women—the right kind of women—we could marry, and then—'

'The right kind?'

'You know what I mean.' Drax shrugged dismissively. 'The dispensable, disposable type—morally decent enough to be acceptable and naïve enough to agree to be divorced with the minimum of fuss and pay-off.'

'Oh, that kind,' Vere said cynically. 'A naïve virgin ready to fall in love with a sheikh and be so grateful to him for marrying her that she willingly accepts being divorced and put aside without wanting a penny. Do they still exist? Somehow I don't think so,' he told Drax dryly. 'Certainly if you could find us such a bride apiece then I would gladly marry mine. But we both know that the kind of woman who would agree to the sort temporary marriage we would want is hardly likely to be the sweet virgin our people would expect. The reality is that she is more likely to be an adventuress, who would demand an extortionate amount of money to go through with a temporary marriage in the first place and who would then probably attempt to sell her story to the press. That kind of media attention would be bound to have a damaging effect on how we are perceived by the rest of the world as men of integrity.' Vere shook his head. 'No, Drax. It sounds like the perfect way out of our current dilemma, but my view is that it would be impossible to find even one woman let alone two of the right type—and fast enough to bring an end to the Ruler's and the Emir's determination to have us marry into their families.'

Drax's eyes gleamed like those of a predatory black panther. 'Is that a challenge, brother?'

Vere laughed. 'I know better than to issue you with any challenges, Drax. But if you can find a woman—'

'*Two* women,' Drax corrected him. 'I promise you I shall find them, Vere. And you shall have the first of them.'

'Mmm…' Vere looked unconvinced. 'Very well. But in the meantime the only way to keep our neighbours at bay is to continue negotiations with the Ruler and the Emir while avoiding making any kind of commitment. The Ruler has invited us to make an unofficial visit to Zuran,' Vere continued. 'And I rather thought you ought to be the one to go, Drax.'

'You mean that the Ruler wants *you* for his sister, since you are the elder,' Drax guessed shrewdly, 'and you want me to put up some delaying tactics. Why not? They want to talk to you in London, by the way,' he told Vere. 'I said that you would be free to fly there for more negotiations once I was back in Dhurahn.'

'One of the benefits of dual rulership—one pair of hands always available to hold onto the helm of leadership here in Dhurahn, no matter what matters of state require our presence elsewhere.'

'But you are the one who prefers to remain here in the desert,' Drax pointed out. 'I am the one who welcomes the cut and thrust of pursuing our business activities elsewhere.'

'A perfect partnership—built on a trust nothing can destroy and absolute loyalty.'

Silently they clasped hands, and then, in the manner of their Arabic ancestors, they exchanged a fierce, brotherly embrace.

CHAPTER ONE

'You are useless—totally and completely useless. I cannot imagine why I ever thought you were up to the demands of this job. You claim to have a degree, and an MBA, and yet you cannot do the simplest thing you are told.'

On and on went the harsh, critical voice of her Lebanese employer, while Sadie dutifully bowed her head beneath the weight of the venom being directed towards her, all too aware that if she looked directly at Madame al Sawar now the other woman would see all too clearly the angry hostility in her own eyes. And Sadie could not afford to give *madame* the opportunity to threaten, as she had done many times already in the two months that Sadie had worked there, to withhold the wages still owing to her.

To be accused so unfairly and so vindictively was bad enough, but to have to stand

here and be berated in a voice loud enough to
carry to the rest of the al Sawar household—
a traditional Arab household, where loss of
face was something to be dreaded and avoided
at all costs—made it even worse. It was typical
of her employer, Sadie recognised, that she
should choose to accost and accuse her while
she was enjoying her legitimate lunch-break in
the peace of the pretty courtyard garden of the
al Sawars' traditional Moorish-style Zuran
home. Sadie knew perfectly well that, although
she could not see them, most of household
staff would be lingering in the shadows of the
building, listening to their employer hectoring
her assistant.

Not that they could *avoid* hearing what was
going on, with *madame* screaming and shout-
ing so loudly. The whole street could probably
hear, Sadie reflected miserably. She wasn't
the only recipient of her employer's vile
temper. Scarcely a day went by without
madame losing her temper with someone.

Sadie could have defended herself against
her employer's unfair accusations, of course,
and told her that she did indeed possess both
a First Class Honours degree and an MBA.
And she could have told her, too, that as much

as Madame al Sawar regretted employing her it couldn't come close to her own regret at having taken the job. But the truth was that she simply couldn't afford to lose this job—not with *madame* having consistently refused to pay her since she came here.

'I have no use for such a deadweight as you in my business. You are dismissed.'

'You can't do that!' Sadie burst out, panicked out of her determination not to be forced into a verbal battle.

'You think not? I assure you that I can. And don't think that you can walk out of here and get another job,' *madame* screeched. 'Because you can't. The Zurani authorities impose very harsh measures on illegals who try to take work from the locals.'

Illegals! Now Sadie *had* to stand up for herself. 'I am not an illegal,' she protested. 'You know that. You assured me yourself when I took this job that all the necessary formalities would be completed on my behalf. I remember signing the necessary forms…' Sadie was beginning to feel slightly sick with panic now, as well as from the heat burning down on her exposed head. She was being made to wait and listen to *madame* ranting in the full burn of the sunlight, whereas *madame* herself remained in the shade.

Sadie could see a smug look of satisfaction in the older woman's eyes as she affected nonchalance with a dismissive shrug.

'I do not remember saying any such thing. And if you try to claim as much now, it will be the worse for you.'

Sadie could hardly believe what she was hearing. She had thought her situation bad enough, but that was nothing to what she was facing now.

With no job, no money, and no legal status here in Zuran her situation was dire indeed. And it had all seemed so promising at the time…

Six months into her first job as an MBA graduate with one of London's premier hedge funds, she had been made redundant to make way for the son of a very senior member of the bank's latest lover. Or that was what she had been told via the office grapevine. It had certainly been easier to swallow that explanation than it had been to accept the jeering comment from one particularly unpleasant male colleague that she was being dumped because she couldn't hack the testosterone-loaded male environment in which she worked.

A top-flight, good, money-earning job in the financial sector—one which would make her completely financially independent—had been her goal all the way through university, and she had initially been devastated by this unwelcome setback to her career plans.

Her parents had divorced when she was in her early teens. Her mother had then married again—a very wealthy man, with children of his own from his first marriage, and with whom she now had a second and younger family. When her mother had first become involved with the man who would become Sadie's stepfather he had lavished time and attention on Sadie, forever telling her now much he wanted her as a daughter. But as soon as her mother had married him he had changed completely towards Sadie, instilling in her the belief that male love, both sexual and paternal, was something that some men could assume to suit themselves.

After her mother's marriage to him Sadie had grown up enduring her stepfather's unkind comments about her father's inability to provide for her as well as he provided for his new children. She had been torn between anger against her parents for divorcing and a protective love for her father, who had remarried as well, and had a young wife and a very young family, and had looked far older and more careworn than his age the last time she had seen him. Unlike her stepfather, her father was not a wealthy man.

It had been pride that had made her refuse to ask for financial help from her stepfather to get through university, and that pride had left her weighed down with a very large student loan. The loss of her first job had meant that she would have to crawl back to her stepfather and ask for his help—help which he had given willingly to his own sons, both of whom had been given a car and an apartment apiece when they had started work—and that was the last thing she had wanted to do.

She could still remember how he had sneered at her when she had announced that she was going to study for her MBA, suggesting that she'd be better off looking for a rich husband to support her instead.

'After all,' had been his comment, 'it isn't as though you haven't got the looks—and the body.'

Yes, she had those. But Sadie had sworn when she had seen the way her obviously highly-sexed stepfather behaved towards her mother, making it plain that he expected her to repay his financial support in bed, that she would never, *ever* let any man think he had the power to demand her sexual compliance just because he paid the bills. Either inside marriage or outside it. And she had stuck to that vow—even though its by-product had been an unexpected and unlooked-for celibacy that had left her partnerless. For Sadie, her financial and sexual independence were strongly interlinked. Thirteen was a very vulnerable age for a girl to witness the kind of relationship Sadie had witnessed between her mother and her stepfather.

When she had seen her current job advertised, in the columns of a national broadsheet newspaper, she had been so excited that she had had to warn herself that there would be hundreds of applicants and that she probably wouldn't stand a chance.

But then, when Monika al Sawar had interviewed her and told her that she specifically wanted to employ a female MBA—'Because my husband is very much the Arab male, and will not tolerate me working one to one with another man'—her hopes had started to rise.

The job Monika had described to her had sounded perfect—challenging and exciting, with plenty of room to grow. Monika's business, she had told Sadie, involved advising new residents to Zuran in the wake of the tourist boom on investment, the buying of Zurani property, and arranging finances for property purchases. Monika had further told Sadie that she wanted a keen young assistant she could train up to work as a financial adviser in her own right.

Sadie had been in seventh heaven when she had got the job—even when the promised business-class flight to Zuran had somehow turned out to be an economy-class flight, and the promised advance of funds to pay a lump sum off her student loan had not materialised.

But then had come the discovery that the accommodation she had been promised was the not the apartment in a modern executive block she had somehow imagined, but instead a very small and basic room in the al Sawar house—and, more disturbingly, that Monika was deducting what seemed to be an overly large sum of money from Sadie's wages to cover her 'bed and board'. Sadie's awkward attempt to discuss her dissatisfaction with this situation had led to the first of the now regular and familiar outbursts of Monika's temper, and with it the withholding of Sadie's wages.

Now, with only a very small sum of money left from the funds she had brought with her, Sadie was getting desperate. Very desperate. But she was not going to let Monika see that.

'Very well, then. I'll go,' Sadie said quietly. 'But not until you have paid me the wages owing to me.'

The scream of fury that erupted from the other woman made Sadie wince, and it could be heard all over the house.

And also outside in the street, where Drax, having parked the hire car he preferred to the Ruler's offer of a chauffeur-driven limousine— mainly because of the privacy it afforded him— was walking towards the house. He slowed his pace to match that of Amar al Sawar. The kindly older man had been a close friend of the twins' father, and neither of them ever visited Zuran without calling to see him. Drax had found him on this occasion at the Royal Palace, and had reluctantly accepted his invitation to return to his home with him. Neither Drax nor Vere liked their father's elderly friend's younger second wife.

'Oh, dear me. I'm afraid it sounds as though Monika is a little upset,' Amar apologised. 'And I had so hoped that this time she would take to the new assistant she hired. Such a delightful young woman. English, and well-educated—a good, kind girl too, modest and sweet-natured.'

If she *was* all of those things then she was certainly no match for Monika, Drax reflected.

'I cannot understand why it is that such an attractive young woman should choose to work instead of marry. If I had a son she is just exactly the kind of girl I would want for him as a wife.'

Now Amar had surprised Drax. The older man was very much of the generation and outlook that followed the old ways and looked for the kind of virtues in a young woman that very few now possessed. Drax suspected that the older man, who was no match for his aggressive wife, deeply regretted having allowed Monika to bully him into marrying her.

From inside the courtyard, the piercing sound of her wrath could still be heard quite plainly by the two men as she berated her young assistant.

'Wages? You expect me to *pay* you for practically ruining my business? Hah!' Monika
screeched at Sadie. '*You* are the one who
should be paying me. Be glad that I am letting
you go without demanding any recompense
from you. If you are wise you will leave now,
this minute, before I change my mind and set
my lawyers to work on you.'

Before Sadie could object Monika had
turned round and begun walking away from
her, leaving her standing in the courtyard.

'My clothes...' she began, too stunned and
battered by Monika's loud ranting and merci-
less tactics for logic or argument. 'My passport...'

'Zuwaina has packed them for you. Take
them and go,' Monika said triumphantly, as
a young maid appeared in the courtyard,
pulling Sadie's case on wheels with one
hand and holding her handbag and passport
in the other.

It gave Sadie a sharp sense of revulsion to
know that Monika had been through her
personal belongings, but the real cause of the
sickness making her feel so clammy and light-
headed was the reality of what she was now
facing. No job, no money, no plane ticket

home. All she could think of to do was throw herself on the mercy of the British Consulate—although it would mean a long walk in to town to get there.

The courtyard gates were being opened and two men were walking through, both of them wearing traditional Arab dress. One of them was the elderly husband of her employer—a charming, educated man who made Sadie think yearningly of the grandfather she could just about remember—while the man with him... Sadie made an involuntary sound deep in her throat, her eyes widening and her heart thudding heavily into her chest wall. The other man was quite simply so compellingly male, and so arrogantly alive with raw sexuality and power, that he was mesmerizing. All Sadie could do was stand there gazing—no, not gazing at him so much as gaping in awe, Sadie mentally derided herself. She who had not only never gaped at a man before, but who had never imagined she would want to do so.

She could feel her face turning pink as he turned his head, so that instead of just seeing his profile she met a full-on swift, hawkish assessment from a pair of narrowed, shockingly unexpected ice-green eyes. Ice-green? Her hands were trembling so much she almost dropped her handbag, grabbing hold of it as it threatened to slip sideways from her grasp.

What was happening to her? Her instinctive and immediate response to her physical reaction was to take refuge in the safety of denial and tell herself that what was happening was caused by her defences having been undermined by Monika's attack on her, not by anything—or anyone—else. But she couldn't escape from the knowledge that with just one glance from those far too knowing green eyes a total stranger had stripped from her the protection with which she had previously kept his sex at bay.

Without saying or doing anything he had broken through her barriers and made her so intensely aware of his male sexual driving force that her whole body was now a mass of chaotic, over-sensitised and far too receptive sexually attuned nerve-endings.

So *this* was physical desire, then! This white-hot unstoppable flood of bitingly intense, dangerously seductive longing mixed with promise, possessing her and dominating everything she was feeling and thinking—

changing her from what she had been into something else as surely as though she had been given into the hands of a sorcerer.

CHAPTER TWO

'ARE you all right, child?'

Sadie could hear the gentle voice of her employer's husband, but somehow it was impossible to drag her imprisoned gaze away from the dangerous, almost cruelly handsome perfection of the man standing beside him. She felt as though she was having to bring herself back up to the clear light of day from the darkest depths of some secret hidden place.

'Yes. Yes, I'm fine,' she managed to gulp—even though she knew that both men must be perfectly aware that she was not.

She risked another look at Professor al Sawar's much younger companion. To her relief, he wasn't searching her soul with that too-intense glittering look any more, and some of the turbulence inside her subsided, allowing her to tell herself that she had over-emphasised his earlier effect on her—no doubt because of the trauma she had just experienced. Relief poured through her like cool, soothing water on over-heated skin.

She could see in the Professor's face that both men had overheard Monika's angry tirade. Her now ex-employer's husband reached into his robe and withdraw a wallet. Normally such an incongruity as the sight of a modern wallet concealed within the folds of such a traditional garment would have made her smile, but now she was struggling too hard to rationalise the rush of unfamiliar sensations seizing her to do anything other than note vaguely that the older man was opening his wallet and withdrawing some money.

'Please—take this…' he was urging her.

Now she *had* to force herself to focus on him.

'I don't know how much my wife owes you, but…'

There was a look in the ice-green eyes that burned her pride. Her reaction was instinctive and immediate. Shaking her head, she stepped back mutely.

'Please…' the Professor was insisting.

'No,' Sadie refused fiercely. Whether his act was a kindness to protect her or a bribe designed to protect his wife, she didn't know; all she did know was that she would not and could not take his money, his charity. She had *earned* her wages, and it was her wages she wanted—not the professor's generosity.

'No,' she repeated in a calmer, more rational tone, even if her voice was shaking slightly. She grabbed hold of her suitcase and hurried towards the still open courtyard gates.

Drax watched her go, protectively shielding the intensity of his desire by lowering his eyelids to hood his focused concentration on her. The familiar, dry, sand-blown scent of the desert in the air he was breathing into his body was sharpened and flooded by the heat of his own arousal. Dismissively he mentally shrugged off the warning his body was activating. He was man, wasn't he? And a man who had perhaps been voluntarily celibate longer than was wise. Drax didn't take women to his bed on sexual impulse. His sense of his position was too strongly developed for that. Actions that potentially shamed him did not just shame him, they shamed Vere—and they shamed the reputation that had been handed down to them. Nevertheless, while it was not his habit to go in for casual serial partner sex, it was perhaps time that he found himself a discreet mistress.

The gates had been closed behind the young woman for several seconds when, as though she had been surreptitiously watching from inside the house, Drax recognised, Monika came into the courtyard, beckoning them both inside. Reluctantly following the Professor, Drax almost missed seeing the small maroon oblong lying on the ground. Bending to pick it up, he frowned when he realised that it was a passport. He opened it, flicking through. Sadie Murray, twenty-five years old, single, light brown eyes, dark blonde almost brown hair, her only distinguishing mark a small mole on the inside of her left thigh…

'Vere—it is always such a pleasure to see you,' Monika was gushing, causing Drax's eyes to narrow as she hurried forward to envelop him in the overpowering strength of her scent. Tucking the passport away, he stepped back from her.

'Sadly for both of us, I'm not Vere,' he told Monika coolly. Over a decade ago, in the early days of her marriage to the Professor, when Drax himself had been a young man in his early twenties, Monika had offered herself to him. She would never forgive him for rejecting her, Drax recognised, and he would never forget that she had so easily planned to betray her husband.

'I appreciate that you have your reasons for doing so, my dear, but, really—that poor child…to dismiss her like that…' the Professor was saying with a worried frown.

'She deserved it,' Monika returned sharply. 'She refused to carry out my instructions with regard to one of my clients, and in doing so cost me a great deal of money.'

'But, my dear, she's so young, and all alone in a foreign country,' the Professor wavered unhappily. 'And morally—'

'Morally? Hah! It is her *morals* that have caused me so much of a problem. Why should I have to suffer the disadvantages of employing a young western woman who has chosen to behave like a traditional virgin?'

'My dear…'

Drax could hear the distress in the older man's voice, but Monika chose to ignore her husband's shock.

Tossing her head, she continued sharply, 'I need a female employee who knows how to *persuade* men to become my clients, not one who freezes them away.'

'Sadie should surely be praised for her virtue, Monika?' the Professor protested.

'I did not employ her for her virtue. She is pretty enough, but plainly she doesn't know how to use that prettiness to her own advantage.' Monika gave a dismissive shrug. 'Now she has to learn the hard way that that does not make good business sense.'

'You have ensured that she has sufficient money to pay for her air ticket home?'

Drax watched as Monika's mouth hardened. 'That is not my concern. If she hasn't, then it will teach her much needed lesson. Let me summon the maid and get her to bring you both some coffee,' she told her husband, determinedly changing the subject.

As a Lebanese woman, Monika lived a far more independent life than that of a traditional Zurani wife, who would never have dreamed of even appearing in front of a male guest of her husband, never mind addressing him directly. She was certainly far too strident for his taste, Drax acknowledged, and he shook his head and refused. 'Not for me, Monika. I'm afraid I can't stay. I have an appointment.'

* * *

It might only be March, but Zuran did not have a spring. Its climate went straight from a welcome 'cool' winter temperature of around twenty-five degrees in February to a swiftly climbing forty-five-degrees-plus in the middle of summer.

For Sadie, having to walk all the way into town with her case, and without the hat she normally wore for protection, the rising temperature felt distinctly too hot. Her hair might be thick and long, its burnished light brunette warmed with natural gold highlights, but it was no protection against the sun. At least she had her sunglasses to shield her eyes from the harshness of the sunlight as it bounced off the white-painted walls of the houses lining the roadside.

No one walked in Zuran—which was no doubt why so many male drivers slowed down as they drove past her. At least, that was what she was going to tell herself, Sadie decided, gritting her teeth as she ignored yet another car driver crawling along beside the kerb, murmuring to her words she was relieved she could not understand before thankfully he drove off when he realised that she had no intention of acknowledging him.

Her dismissal was so unfair. She had been

good at her job, she knew that, but no way had she intended to coax and tease men into signing up with Monika by hinting at providing them with a sexual reward that she was not going to deliver. Sadie loathed that kind of female behaviour, and she loathed even more the kind of men who expected it.

Perhaps she was naïve, but it had shocked her to discover that a female employer should expect it of her—especially out here in this predominantly morally conservative part of the world. About her reaction to the man who had been accompanying Monika's elderly husband she did not want to think at all.

Drax was just about to put his foot down to join the fast lane of traffic when the car phone rang. He knew it would be Vere calling him. It was typical of Drax that he never questioned why or how he should know that without looking at his phone. It was just an accepted part of their twinship.

'How did the meeting go with the Ruler?' Vere asked.

'Well enough—although I don't think he was too pleased that I turned up in your place. And, speaking of people who weren't as pleased to see me as they would have been to see you, I've just seen the Professor. Monika asked to be remembered to you.'

'So you've been too busy to find me a wife, I take it?' Vere responded, ignoring Drax's dig about Monika.

Up ahead of him, in the dust of the roadside, Drax could see the lone figure of a young woman walking and dragging her suitcase behind her. She looked weary—forlorn, almost.

What was it Amar has said about her? That she was modest, the kind of young woman he would be happy to see his son marry. Drax remembered the passport he had picked up. By rights he should have handed it over to the al Sawars, because the girl would surely return there to look for it once she realised she had lost it.

She certainly wasn't greedy, he acknowledged. He had seen that with his own eyes. And she *had* to be naïve if she'd let herself be persuaded into working for Monika.

'Drax? Are you still there?'

'Yes, I'm still here, Vere. As to your bride— well, that's where you are wrong, my brother. It just so happens that I may have found you the perfect temporary wife.'

Drax switched off his phone before Vere could say anything, and then started to cut the speed of his car.

Sadie could hear the now familiar tell-tale sound of a car braking to a crawl just behind her, but she refused to look round. However, this car didn't pull away as quickly as the others had when she did not respond. Instead it continued to keep pace with her, casting a long shadow in front of her. She tried to walk a little bit faster, wishing she could move away from the side of the road, but the land beyond was too rough for her to wheel her case over it.

There was no need for her to panic, she assured herself. It was broad daylight and, even if he was being more persistent than the others, surely whoever it was would soon get bored when she didn't respond, soon put his foot down to race past her in a cloud of sandy dust.

Only he didn't. And out of the corner of her eye she could see a long black bonnet edging just ahead of her, then keeping pace with her.

She couldn't walk any faster; she was panting slightly already, her skin soaked with perspiration caused not just by the heat now but by her anxiety as well.

'Ms Murray?'

Hearing her name spoken in crisp accent-free English gave her such a shock that she froze. Just as he had estimated she would, she reflected bitterly several seconds later, when the car stopped, the driver's door opened and the driver himself stepped out in front of her, trapping her between his body and his car.

'You!'

Why had she said that? It had sounded so personal and so betraying somehow—as though she were deliberately creating an intimacy between them. And that hadn't been her intention. She was just so shocked to see the man she had last seen standing in the Al Sawars' courtyard with her employer's husband standing in front of her.

Unlike her, he wasn't wearing sunglasses, and something about the look she could see in his eyes made her feel like some poor creature of the desert caught in the predatory searching stare of a falcon.

'If Madame Al Sawar asked you to come after me...' she began uncertainly.

Before she could finish what she was saying Drax silenced her with a swift frown.

'I can acquit you because you do not know me well enough to know that I do not act as an errand boy for others,' he told her arrogantly. 'But do you really know Monika so little that you think she'd show that kind of remorse?'

Sadie looked away from him. He was right, of course. Monika was not the type to suffer from second thoughts, much less guilt over what she had done.

'I came after you because there is something I want to discuss with you. The Professor speaks very highly of you. He considers you to be a young woman of good morals and intelligence.' Drax was not going to tell her that the Professor had also confirmed his own assessment that she was more inclined to think the best of others than the worst, and that this made her vulnerable to the selfish machinations of the unscrupulous.

Sadie could feel a pink flush heating her face as she listened to this praise.

'You are fully qualified to work in the financial services industry, so I understand?'

His question startled Sadie. 'I have a degree and an MBA,' she acknowledged. She could see Drax nodding his head, as though her words had confirmed what he already knew.

'It could be that I can offer you a job to replace the one you have just lost.'

Now he could see uncertainty and suspicion in her eyes, along with the kind of female wariness that made Drax congratulate himself again on his own intuition. She would be perfect for the plan he had outlined to his twin.

Sadie looked at him with a challenging expression. She wasn't so naïve that she wasn't aware that there was a certain type of Arab male who looked to western women to satisfy his sexual needs via a series of brief sex-only liaisons.

'Thank you, but my plan has always been to return to the UK to work.'

'But not without the money to pay your fare or your passport?' Drax suggested.

Her passport? Sadie looked at him, and then looked down at her bag. But there was no need for her to look inside it, because Drax was already holding her passport in his hand.

'What…?'

'Why don't you get in the car?' Drax looked at his watch. 'I can tell you about the job that's on offer over a late lunch in the city.'

Did he really expect her to fall for that kind of line? She wasn't that naïve. 'I'm sorry, but I'm not interested—in anything,' she emphasised firmly, reaching for her passport.

Drax stepped back from her, sliding her passport out of sight somewhere within the folds of his dishdasha.

'Very well,' he said calmly, and turned back to his car.

'My passport...' Sadie protested frantically.

'What passport? If, when I reach the airport for my return flight to Dhurahn, I find that I still have the passport I found lying on the ground in Zuran City, then I shall naturally see that it reaches the nearest British Embassy.'

'What?' This was getting worse by the minute. Not only had he got her passport, he was also planning to leave the country. 'No, you can't do that!' Sadie told him wildly.

'No?' The ice-green eyes had hardened.

Ignoring the warning in them, Sadie tried to grab her passport back from him, crying out as she stumbled over a sharp piece of rock jutting out of the earth and then fell heavily against Drax.

Drax's reactions were quicker than Sadie's. He caught her easily, and could have held her away from him so their bodies didn't come into contact, but for some reason he wasn't prepared to explain to himself he didn't. Instead, he wrapped his hands around her upper arms to steady her, and let her body rest against his own. He could feel the soft rounded swell of her breasts, and the temptation to slide his hands from her arms to her hips, to pull her more intimately against him, was so strong and instinctive that it startled him. She smelled hot and sweet, and her scent caused an unexpected surge of sexual awareness to grip him. It took him off guard.

What the hell *was* this? He didn't normally react with this kind of easy arousal. A man in his position had to be careful about his sexual liaisons. Drax had learned that long ago. He had a responsibility towards the position he held. He and Vere had a shared duty to give their subjects a good example and to set high moral standards. Casual sex wasn't something he indulged in, and yet here he was so stiffly erect that he felt downright uncomfortable— and all on account of this dusty young woman with her topaz eyes and her pale skin. A woman he had already decided to offer to his brother.

Which was, of course, why he was testing her moral standards. If she took advantage of their shared intimacy now to come on to him he would know there was no point in pursuing his plan. Neither could he afford to become sexually involved with her—it wasn't for sex that he wanted her. She must be proved to be the kind of woman the Professor believed her to be. The kind of woman who was the opposite of women like Monika al Sawar and who would not try to institute sex with a man without being invited to do so.

After Sadie's shock at being so unexpectedly close to Drax, with all its drugging excitement, came recognition of her vulnerability—and with it panic.

'Let go of me!' She sounded more pleading than assertive, Sadie recognised weakly, as she heard the emotion in her own voice. Being this close to this man wasn't good for her, she admitted. It reactivated everything she had felt in the courtyard, and underlined her inability to override her physical response to him.

So why wasn't she doing more to make him release her? Why, in fact, was she leaning into him as though she couldn't stand without the support of his body? Did she really not care

about the danger of her own actions? Not just
via the casual sex with a stranger he might
think she was inviting but, just as dangerously,
via the effect her proximity to him was having
on what she had always believed to be givens
about herself. Givens like the fact that she
wasn't a woman who had strong sexual urges;
like the fact that she wasn't a woman who
could ever be overwhelmed by desire for a
man just by looking at him; like the fact that
she was far too sensible to take risks with her
sexual and emotional health.

It was the heat of the sun that was making
her feel weak, she hurried to reassure herself.
Nothing else. She certainly wasn't entertain-
ing the kind of fantasies she had heard some
western women had about sexy Arab
sheikhs—even if this man was everything that
such a man should be, right down to the aura
of danger surrounding him.

'This is Zuran,' she heard him telling her
coldly as he thrust her away. 'Here it is not acceptable for a man and a woman to embrace
in public, no matter what you may be used to
doing elsewhere!'

What *she* might be used to doing elsewhere?
He was making it sound as though he thought

she was coming on to him. Mortified, Sadie pulled away from him and stepped back. She was right about one thing. She *had* been out in the hot sun for longer than was wise, and her own sudden movement had caused a wave of faintly nauseating dizziness to swamp her.

The sight of Sadie's suddenly too pale face accompanied by her soft gasp of shock had Drax reacting with instinctive speed as he recognised the onset of heat sickness. He bundled her into the car so quickly that Sadie didn't have time to do anything more than make an incoherent protest. She could feel the car depressing as he slid into the driver's seat and switched on the engine. She could hear too the sound of the doors locking as he set the car in motion and pulled away from the kerb.

'Stop,' she said frantically. 'You can't do this!'

'What would you have preferred me to do—leave you where you were to suffer sunstroke?'

'There's plenty of shade in the city.'

'You would never have made it that far,' Drax told her bluntly, before adding, 'And you needn't look at me like that. You have nothing to fear from me.'

'That's easy for you to say,' Sadie retorted shakily. 'You've practically kidnapped me, and—'

'And now you're worried that I might be carrying you off to my harem to have my wicked way with you?' Drax mocked her, raising one dark eyebrow. 'Do you really think that's likely? Let's be honest with one another—in today's world, if I wanted to indulge myself sexually with a disposable partner I would hardly need to kidnap one, would I?'

Her eyes were the colour of clear warm honey, Drax noticed, her tawny hair as polished and silken as the coat of one of his cherished pure-bred Arab mares. He sensed within her the same pride that possessed his falcons—a pride he had the power and the skill to tame, so that they came to his hand as softly, as though they were doves.

Her skin was too pale, though, for the harshness of the desert's midday sun, and she was paying for her folly in ignoring that fact now. Perspiration beaded her forehead and her head drooped on the slender stem of her neck. Drax guessed that in addition to her obvious apprehension at being bundled into his car she was probably also feeling slightly nauseous. She was certainly likely to be dehydrated.

He reached out and tapped open the centre console that separated their seats. 'You will find a bottle of water in here. Take it and drink some,' he advised her sternly.

Water! Until he had spoken she hadn't realised how thirsty she was. Sadie's tongue-tip flicked against the dry saltiness of her lips as she reached eagerly for the unopened bottle.

Removing the top, she lifted the bottle towards her mouth.

The traffic was heavy enough for Drax to slow down and watch her. Her lips were soft and full, and as she closed them around the head of the bottle she also closed her eyes, as though she was giving herself over to a much longed-for sensory pleasure. She drank quickly, the muscles of her throat contracting and expanding as she swallowed and then drank more deeply.

The arousal Drax had felt earlier returned, thrusting past the barriers of civility and necessity. Was she aware of just how intensely erotic her actions were? Drax wondered, as between one breath and the next he became trapped within the sexual urgency and immediacy of

PENNY JORDAN   51

the images his own brain was creating from
her actions. Inside his head the soft fullness of
her lips clung eagerly not to the water bottle
but to his flesh, greedily absorbing its texture
and taste. A pothole in the road caused water
from the bottle to trickle from her lips down
her throat and beyond, filling the hollow at its
base and then spilling from it. If he were to lap
its wetness from her skin now it would taste
of her flesh and her heat, and the taste would
feed his tongue to taste her more intimate
wetness, to…

The sudden sharp blare of a car horn somewhere up ahead of them wrenched Drax out
of his fantasy and back to reality. His heart
was the thudding in slow, heavy erotic beats
as it urged his body to greater arousal. He
reached for his own bottle of water, and drank
fiercely from it, as though to quench the heat
of what he was experiencing.

The air-conditioning was on, so why was
she suddenly feeling aware of a heat so
physical that it not only seemed to be filling
the interior of the car, it also felt as if it was
actually touching her, pressing against her skin
as though in a caress? Because she wanted to
be caressed? By him? What kind of craziness

had possessed her? Was this some kind of heat-induced lust that was a by-product of too much exposure to the sun? Sadie's thoughts spilled dizzily on top of one another, blocking her rational exit from them. She fought valiantly against them, making herself focus on the scenery outside the car.

'We're almost in the city,' she told Drax. 'It's kind of you to think about offering me a job, but really there's no need. If you give me my passport and drop me off—'

'You're rejecting the job without knowing what it is?'

Sadie's words had aroused two very different and competing instant reactions inside Drax—one, that he should stop the car, give her the passport and forget that he had ever seen her; the other that there was no way he was going to let her go.

He pressed harder on the accelerator, swinging the car into the outer lane that led away from the city.

CHAPTER THREE

'As JOINT rulers of Dhurahn, my brother and I have for some considerable time been looking into ways to provide our country and our people with a prosperous future once our oil runs out.'

Did he really expect her to believe that *he* was a ruler of Dhurahn? She had heard of Zuran's neighbouring state, but she had also seen the protocol and the hierarchy of personnel that attended Zuran's Ruler whenever he left the palace.

'To this end, as you may know, we have developed an agricultural policy that has led to us provide other Gulf States with fresh produce. That is all well enough in its own way, but my brother and I both believe that we need something more. To effect this we have been in negotiation for some time now with various organisations in the City of London, with a view to establishing a business and financial centre of excellence within Dhurahn.'

Sadie started to frown. She *had* heard vague rumours of something like this, she acknowledged. In the way of such things word had got out of this ambitious plan by an unnamed gulf state, and she had also heard the young male MBAs with whom she'd worked stating that if the plan went ahead it would be a golden opportunity for the ambitious.

'My brother and I are now at a stage in our negotiations where we are looking to put together a team of young MBAs to work with the experts we'll be bringing in to implement our plans. Professor al Sawar, who was a longstanding friend of our late father, speaks very highly of you, and naturally it occurred to me that you would be an ideal candidate for our team.'

Drax gave a small shrug. 'Of course I appreciate that offering you a job in this manner is not exactly orthodox business procedure, but events have moved ahead with more speed than we had anticipated. Interviewing and selecting a large number of the right young graduates and MBAs is going to take time. We have therefore decided to set up a small, specially selected team with all speed. The fact that you are here in Zuran and in need of a job makes you an ideal candidate for a place on that team.

'Time is very much of the essence here. My brother has to leave for London for further negotiations, and I need to return to our country to allow him to do so, since one of us must always be resident in Dhurahn. If I can take you back with me and set you to work, initially as my PA with regard to the preliminary paperwork and the setting up of procedures and negotiations, that will allow me to have more time to work on other aspects of this ground breaking project.

'You will be well paid. My brother and I have already agreed upon a salary scale for our young graduates—it is almost double the best rate paid in London, and I assure you that you *will* be paid. As rulers of Dhurahn our word is our bond, and we do not operate the same kind of business ethics as Monika al Sawar.'

'You don't really expect me to believe that you're a ruler of Dhurahn, do you?' Sadie challenged him. Just what kind of idiot did he take her for?

'You're accusing me of lying to you? Why should I bother to do that?'

'Rulers of Arab states don't drive themselves around without escorts, or—'

'You know this for a fact, do you? So, how many rulers of Arab States exactly are you familiar with? Have you any idea just how insulting you are being?' he asked Sadie softly. 'Under traditional Dhurahni law people can be locked away for the rest of their life for such an insult to a member of its Ruling Family. In ancient times they would have had their tongue cut out so that they could never speak another lie. That was if they were allowed to live.'

Sadie shuddered, sickened by the graphic image he was forcing on her. He was certainly every inch the haughty all-powerful potentate whose word was absolute law, she admitted, wishing now that she had not spoken out so rashly.

'I do not lie, Ms Murray. I do not need to. I could drive back to Zuran City and take you to the Ruler to verify my identity for you. Indeed, I could ask the same of your own Embassy. But I don't have time. I need to return to Dhurahn before my brother leaves.'

Sadie saw the look in his eyes as his mouth curled downwards in hard dismissal, and knew that he meant what he said.

It was still hard for to take what he was saying at face value—especially after she had been so naïvely taken in by Monika.

'I find it hard to accept that you're willing to offer me a job without knowing anything about me, or—'

'Here in the Gulf we believe very strongly in fate. It is true that when I left the Royal Palace earlier today with Professor al Sawar the thought of employing you or anyone else was not something I had planned. However, a clever man does not ignore the opportunities that fate offers to him.' Drax gave another shrug. That was certainly what he believed, even if the opportunity he believed 'fate' had given him on this particular occasion was not the one he was now promoting to Sadie Murray.

'A contract will be drawn up that allows us both a probationary period in which to assess the consequences of what might seem to be a too-hasty decision. I have no desire to keep you in my country against your will. An unwilling worker is of no benefit to Dhurahn. As co-rulers of Dhurahn, both my brother and I are well aware of that. Neither of us would ever tolerate anything that prejudices the progress or the reputation of our country. And, just for the record, I have no desire to keep you in my bed unwillingly, where the same principle applies. I see no pleasure to be gained in a woman who is not there of her own free will and her own desire.'

Sadie was struggling to get her head around not just what Drax was saying but also the whole *Arabian Nights* fantasy of being told by the ruler of a Gulf State that he wanted to whisk her off to his kingdom.

However, his purpose in taking her there was not because he wanted her to give him one thousand and one nights of pleasure, as Scheherazade had given her Caliph master with her fabulous stories, but—far more mundanely—so that he could use her expertise to help build a world-class knowledge economy with a world-class financial exchange to rival those of London, New York and Hong Kong. If what she was being told was the truth…

Surely rulers travelled in cavalcades of cars, surrounded by courtiers and security men? They did not drive themselves around in ordinary, if up-market, saloon cars. The ease with which Monika had deceived her still stung. This man—Drax, as she recalled hearing the Professor call him—might physically possess the kind of arrogance that went with high estate, but that did not mean he actually was what he claimed to be.

'I…it all sounds so far-fetched,' she told him doubtfully.

The green eyes glittered a look over her that was a combustible mixture of savage fury and arrogant disbelief.

'You *dare* to persist in trying to accuse me of being a liar?'

'I have a right to protect myself from being tricked into another situation in which I end up being out of pocket,' Sadie defended herself. 'There is a saying—"If a man makes a fool of me once, shame on him. If twice, shame on me." You *say* you are a co-ruler of Dhurahn.'

'I say it because that is what I am,' he retorted. 'I am not Monika al Sawar. I *am* co-Ruler of Dhurahn, with a moral responsibility towards my brother to act in a way that cannot possibly leave any stain on his honour, just as he has that responsibility to me.'

So much had happened in such a short space of time, the changes in her circumstances had been so seismic, that Sadie suspected she wasn't in any fit state to make any kind of decision—never mind one as potentially reckless as agreeing to accept the job she was being offered.

And yet what alternative did she really have? She had no money, no family in the true sense to love and support her in England, should she choose to return, no job to return to there, and no passport to return there with, thanks to the man seated next to her, she reminded herself grimly. And what kind of message did that give her—the fact that he was prepared to use such an underhand method to force her to do as he wished?

'What if I choose not to accept your offer?' she demanded.

Drax could hear the uncertainty in her voice. As though he could see into her head, he could imagine her thoughts. She had come to the Gulf in order to change her life in some way; that desire would still exist, despite Monika al Sawar's behaviour towards her.

'Why would you do that?' he asked her coolly. 'Dhurahn can match everything that Zuran can offer you and exceed it. You would be a fool not to accept. And since I have offered you a job, and I do not offer jobs to fools, you cannot be one.'

Such arrogance. It was breathtaking. And exciting? Was she excited by it? By him? Thoughts she had never imagined were whirling through her head like grains of sand being whipped up by the desert wind, to create a mesmerizing, whirling force that changed the known to the unknown.

This man—powerful sheikh or lying braggart—possessed that same power as the dessert wind, and for better or for worse she was being swept into the maelstrom of excitement and uncertainty he was creating within her.

If he was speaking the truth then surely she would be a fool to turn down this kind of opportunity? Especially now, with no earnings to show for her time in Monika's employ and the burden of her student loan still hanging over her.

'If I take this job you are offering me, there will be two conditions,' she told him firmly.

She was attempting to *bargain* with him? A woman? Powerless, jobless, trapped in his car, and wholly at his mercy? She was either very foolish or very brave. Vere would appreciate neither of those qualities. He was a fair man, but very autocratic. Whereas he...

He, Drax admitted to himself, was not always fair and autocratic—only when it suited him. Vere often teased him that he was Machiavellian. Drax preferred to think that he understood people and their weaknesses.

'And those conditions are?'

Sadie took a deep breath.

'That you return my passport to me and that you pay me—*before* we leave for Dhurahn—an advance on my salary sufficient to pay for a return ticket to the UK.'

So she had learned something from working for Monika after all.

'Certainly.'

Sadie looked at him uncertainly, wondering if she had misheard his prompt and affirmative response.

'You agree?' she questioned him.

'I'm beginning to see why Monika found it so easy to manipulate you,' Drax told her. 'A good negotiator behaves as though he or she believes themselves to be in an unassailably strong position even if they know that they are not.'

His instincts about her had been right. There was a softness, a vulnerability about her, that would make her perfect for his plans. The fact that in asking for an advance of her salary all she had asked for was the price of her air ticket home added to his confidence in his own intuition.

'Yes, I agree—but with a condition of my own. And that is that while I am prepared to advance you the money you require before we leave Zuran, I am not prepared to return your passport to you until we reach Dhurahn. Still, you have at least shown some initiative—and I must say that I am impressed that you believe you are in a position to make conditions,' Drax told Sadie smoothly.

'And I am amazed that you would want someone working for you who was not aware of their value,' Sadie countered. When his eyebrows lifted and she saw the cynicism in his eyes, she added swiftly, 'The fact that Monika cheated me out of my wages does not lessen the value of my qualifications.'

'I agree. But it does raise questions about your judgement. Academic qualifications on their own are all very well, but the shrewdest and most successful entrepreneurs will admit that it is the instincts they have honed and come to rely on that create the alchemic effect to turn the base metal of mere scholarship into the pure gold of financial genius. And that, surely, is true of every sphere of achievement?'

'You are the one who offered me a job, not the other way around,' Sadie felt bound to remind him.

But instead of responding to the anger in her voice Drax changed the subject, demanding coolly, 'Monika's accusations against you interest me. What exactly did she mean?'

His question had caught her off guard. Sadie looked away from him, not wanting him to see her naked expression and read in it what she would prefer to keep hidden.

'She wanted me to…to persuade her clients that certain investments were of better value and more promising than she knew them to be.'

A tactful and evasive answer, Drax acknowledged. But, knowing Monika as he did, it wasn't one he had any difficulty in interpreting.

'She wanted you to use your sexual allure to sell unsafe investments, you mean?' he suggested. It was no less than he had worked out for himself, but it interested him to witness her obvious discomfort in talking about it. Because she had felt obliged to give in to Monika's bullying?

Drax's good humour evaporated. A woman who had sold herself sexually, even if she had been forced to do so by someone else, was not the kind of woman who could become the wife of a ruler of Dhurahn—even in a marriage that was to be both temporary and unconsummated.

When Sadie didn't say anything his mouth compressed. The light mockery disappeared from his voice as he demanded, far more sharply, 'It was only sexual allure she expected you to use, I trust? And not something more intimate…?'

'There was a suggestion from her that I might flatter some of the clients a little more than I felt was morally acceptable,' Sadie told him reluctantly. He was, after all, a friend of Monika's husband, even if he had made it plain that he did not like Monika herself.

'She wanted you to have sex with her clients in return for them giving her their business? Is that what you mean?'

'She never said that in as many words, but it was plain enough what she expected me to do.'

'And did you?'

Sadie was too outraged to think of being tactful.

'*No*. I did not. That is *not* the way I live my life,' she told him furiously. 'And it never will be. So if you are thinking of suggesting that I—'

He stopped the car with such force that she was thrown against her seatbelt.

'*What?* You would dare to suggest that I, a ruler of Dhurahn, would sink to such depths?'

Sadie could see how much she had offended him. Where before she had seen arrogance, now she could see a fierce, steely pride.

'I wasn't making any accusations. I was simply stating what I am not prepared to do,' Sadie defended herself.

She was speaking the truth. Drax could see that. Everything was as he had hoped—and expected. She was perfect for Vere, and he was a genius for having found her—and for having seized the opportunity she afforded so swiftly and effectively, he congratulated himself.

He turned his attention back to the road, setting the car in motion again.

'So it is agreed that you will accept the job I have offered you and will return with me to Dhurahn?'

Was it? Sadie hadn't given any verbal

agreement to do anything, but somehow she wasn't able to say as much to him. And she couldn't really blame him for taking her silence as a sign that she had accepted what he had said, she acknowledged, when several minutes later he told her, 'We should be at the airport in less than half an hour.'

'I'll need my passport,' Sadie felt bound to point out.

The look he gave her reduced her to immediate silence.

'We will be returning to Dhurahn in my own private jet. Naturally, as an employee I have personally appointed, there will be no need for you to go through passport control either in Zuran or Dhurahn.'

However, he would have to telephone the palace and make his excuses to Zwar's Ruler for returning to Dhurahn at such short notice, Drax acknowledged.

His own private jet. Sadie struggled not to look too overwhelmed.

'I am not sure…er… That is… I'm afraid I don't know your correct title or how I should address you,' she managed to say uncertainly.

He gave a small shrug of the powerful shoulders she had already noticed.

'My brother and I both had a very liberal up-bringing. Our mother was Irish and our father wanted us to follow in his footsteps and be educated in England and Paris. While the traditionalists in our country still use our titles, since we are modelling our new venture on modern lines everyone will be on first-name terms with one another. Therefore you will address me as Drax.

'Drax…'

She made his name sound as though she was tasting it—a soft whisper of sound as her lips parted round the 'D' and then closed softly on the 'x'.

'It is a family name,' he told her dismissively, irritated with himself for the images that were forming inside his head. He had seen far more beautiful women and had known far more sensually explicit and carnal women—so what was it about this woman that uniquely invested so much of what she said with such an intense sensuality that just being with her had his body in an almost constant state of arousal? It was a reaction to her he would have to destroy, since it was Vere who would have the right to claim her sexually—if he chose to do so.

The sudden savage surge of male possessiveness that gripped him made him frown. He was engaged in a matter of great diplomatic importance—one that must not be prejudiced by some ill-considered sexual lust. He had been too long without a woman. That was all that was causing him to feel desire for her, Drax reassured himself. It was over a year since he had ended his last relationship, and it was no wonder that his body was reminding him of its needs.

There was a very discreet and elegant retired belly dancer who had returned to Dhurahn after the death of her elderly husband and would be more than glad to welcome him into her bed, and she understood the rules that would govern their relationship without him having to spell them out to her. She was only just thirty, and stunningly beautiful.

They were at the airport. Sadie felt her stomach muscles start to clench. Was she doing the right thing? Was it too late for her to change her mind?

Change *her* mind? So far all the decisions had been made for her, not by her, Sadie forced herself to admit. And yet, if she was honest with herself, there was something exciting and energising about the thought of the career challenge that now lay ahead of her. If he—*Drax*—this Arabian sheikh who had swept into her life like the hot desert wind and taken her over, was telling her the truth.

CHAPTER FOUR

ZURAN airport was world-famous for its elegance and the number of shops in its duty-free shopping mall.

A snap of his fingers and a few quiet words from Drax had ensured that they were ushered through the airport's security system by Zurani officials, and her case had been politely but firmly taken from her.

Without knowing quite how it had happened, Sadie discovered that she was obliged to walk behind her new employer, following in his wake as he strode arrogantly through the brightly lit mall with its designer label shops. He spoke into his mobile phone in Arabic, holding a conversation with someone who made him laugh several times. A woman? Sadie wondered. *His* woman?

The ferocity of the sensation that spiked through her shocked her into stopping abruptly, and it took the hasty apology of someone bumping into her to break her out of the paralysis that had seized her. It wasn't quite so easy to move her thoughts on. Why on earth had the thought of a man she hardly knew having a sexual relationship with another woman stopped her in her tracks and filled her with such a fierce surge of envy? *Envy?* That wasn't what she had felt at all, she hastily denied to herself.

She needed to find something else to focus her thoughts on. Determinedly, she looked around the impressive terminal hallway.

Huge gold palm trees reached up the full three floors of what was claimed to be the world's biggest and most exclusive duty-free airport shopping mall. Tiny sparkling lights illuminated the trunks and the leaves, and beneath her feet the marble floor was immaculately clean. Everywhere she looked she could see evidence of Zuran's wealth and status—and that of the travellers filling the mall. Being here reminded Sadie of how she had planned to treat herself to a few new things before returning home, thinking that the salary Monika had agreed to pay her would allow her some small indulgences.

Her wardrobe badly needed revamping; that was for sure. The cheap business clothes she had bought for her first job were now worn and shabby, and not really suited to the Gulf's hot climate. Monika had promised her that she would provide her with a working wardrobe of clothes on her arrival in Zwar, but as with everything else the promised new clothes had never materialised. Now, looking at the displays in the windows of the shops lining the mall bearing the exclusive logos of well-known high-profile designers, and being surrounded by elegantly dressed women, Sadie couldn't help giving a small sigh. She was not a materialistic person, but she still paused wistfully to look towards the windows, all too aware of how unfavourably she compared to both the mannequins in the shops and the women around her.

Yes, it would have been fun to treat herself to some new clothes. Fun, but now, thanks to Monika, impossible, she told herself sturdily. She quickened her pace to catch up with her new employer, the co-Ruler of Dhurahn—she still wasn't sure she would be able to get used to addressing him informally as Drax. She just hoped that she was doing the right thing, that she wasn't jumping out of one bad situation into another that was potentially even worse—because it was obvious to her that she couldn't change her mind now. Drax had her passport and she had no money.

Up ahead of them several small electric buggies were waiting.

'These will take us to the Royal runway,' Drax informed her matter-of-factly as he was ushered into the first buggy. Accompanied by the same officials who had escorted them through the airport, Sadie had to travel behind him.

A group of uniformed and robed officials were waiting to receive them when the buggies came to a halt, and Sadie watched as the waiting men salaamed respectfully to Drax, who in turn merely inclined his head, indicating that there was no question of who was the highest ranking person there.

An immaculate strip of beautiful carpet ran from the exit to the foot of the steps leading up to a gleaming jet waiting on the tarmac, and overhead a canopy had been erected to protect them from the sun. This was travelling as Sadie had never experienced it before.

The robed officials surrounded Drax, their

dark silk cloaks billowing in the wind as they escorted him to the plane. Sadie's escort consisted of a small group of men dressed in white tunics, traditional baggy trousers and richly embroidered waistcoats bearing the device of the Royal Ruling Family of Zuran. One of them was carrying her shabby case. She felt as though she had stepped into some kind of parallel but very unfamiliar world, and if she was honest she was beginning to feel completely overwhelmed by it.

Several smartly uniformed men, who looked as though they must be the pilots and crew, were waiting at the bottom of the steps to the aircraft. Like the officials, they too bowed respectfully to Drax, and Sadie caught an unmistakably Australian twang in the voice of one of them as he murmured respectfully, 'Highness.'

As Drax started to mount the steps, Sadie hung back. It was almost as though she didn't exist, as though he had forgotten all about her. Her throat had gone tight, and suddenly she felt very alone and forlorn.

As though somehow he had sensed what she was feeling, Drax turned round to look at her. Although he didn't say a word, somehow

Sadie found that she was climbing the steps towards him, as though compelled to do so by some power that was emanating from him. There was something in the commanding intensity of those green eyes that exerted as much of a pull on her senses as any magician from an Arabian fairytale might have done. A man like this could be dangerous to know for a woman like her, an inner voice warned her, but Sadie refused to listen to it. This was the twenty-first century, and she was far too much of a modern woman to let herself drift off into some foolish fantasy about powerful, sensual desert men and their effect on her sex.

Assuming a businesslike expression, she followed Drax into the plane. Inside, the jet was nothing like any aircraft she had ever flown in before. There were no rows of seats. Instead there was a large open space, its walls painted a subtle shade of blue-grey and its floor covered in off-white carpet. Several very modern-looking leather chairs were artfully placed around the space, which also held a large black desk with a computer, on which Drax was already working.

A uniformed steward came towards her, guiding her to a chair. 'There is a TV screen concealed in the wall opposite you,' he told her, offering her a handset and earphones. 'And on the opposite side of the dividing screen you will find a guest bedroom and bathroom, should you wish to rest in private. However, the flight time to Dhurahn is only one hour, and I shall be serving champagne and canapés before we take off, followed by a meal. If you have any dietary preferences…?'

'No, none,' Sadie answered, trying to perch upright on the edge of the leather chair in a businesslike manner, resisting the temptation to subside into its luxurious comfort. There was something about its shaping that invited the human body to abandon itself into a languorously sensual pose that she didn't feel was appropriate for an employee on probation.

Putting an automatically dialled call through to his brother, Drax swung round to look at her while he waited for Vere to answer. She looked uncertain and slightly over-whelmed. That was good. He wanted to ensure that he kept the upper hand, and the slight apprehension she was betraying reinforced his confidence in what he was doing. He was pretty sure she didn't speak Arabic, but just in case he swung back to face his desk, away from her, keeping his voice low as he answered Vere's, 'Yes, Drax?'

'I am just about to leave Zuran, Vere, and I am returning with a very special gift for you. Perhaps it will give you a hint as to what it is when I tell you that its price is above rubies.' When his brother made no response Drax added softly, 'I have found you the perfect temporary wife, and I am bringing her back to Dhurahn with me.'

'*What?*'

Drax laughed. 'It is true. I have found you a wife, Vere, and she is perfect for our purpose. Wait until you see her.'

'Seeing her is all I shall have time for, Drax. I am leaving for London as soon as you are back.'

Vere had sounded more incredulous than pleased by his news, Drax admitted when the call ended. He frowned as he looked across at Sadie, who was still struggling to sit upright in a chair that was designed for reclining. She looked unsure of herself, and slightly stressed. His brother was a man who liked elegant, im-maculate women—and, no matter how perfect she might be in other ways, as far as her personal appearance went she was not dressed or groomed in a way that would appeal to Vere.

Sensing that she was being watched, Sadie looked toward Drax, colouring up when she saw the way he was scrutinising her. It was not a flattering look she was being given—quite the opposite—and her face started to burn.

'I have some business to attend to before we take off,' Drax told her. 'But it won't take more than half an hour. Beyond this office there is a private suite, which includes a bedroom and a bathroom.'

'Yes, I know. The steward has already told me that,' Sadie interrupted him hurriedly, wondering if she looked as flustered and uncomfortable as she felt. The truth was that she simply wasn't used to sexy, powerful men telling her in drawling, wickedly sensual voices about bedrooms and bathrooms being on hand, should she require them.

The now familiar lift of one dark eyebrow signalled its owner's disdainful reaction to her interruption.

'Excellent. I appreciate that you left the al Sawars' in some haste, and that you may wish to refresh yourself and change your clothes prior to our arrival in Dhurahn, when I hope to be able to introduce you to my brother before he leaves for London. Ali will show you where everything is, and bring your bag to you, should you need it. And now, if you will excuse me, I must attend to a small matter of business I have overlooked.'

He was leaving her here alone on the plane? She had to fight not to spring up and cling to him, begging not to be abandoned. Abandoned? By a man she barely knew? She was being totally ridiculous.

But he had taken control of her life, Sadie recognised as Ali salaamed him out of the doorway, and received another of those regal inclinations of Drax's dark head in response. And in doing so he had thrust her into a kind of lifestyle in which she felt totally alien and insecure.

And was she being over-sensitive, or had he been hinting that she looked as though she was in need of a change of clothes? He had mentioned that she would meet his brother. Meet him, or be inspected and then potentially rejected by him because of her appearance? Did it matter if she was? The extent to which she felt mortified by the thought of being considered not smart enough to work for the

Rulers of Dhurahn told her that it did. And yet hadn't she always despised the attitude of men like her stepfather, who judged others on their outer appearance and their material possessions?

There was a big difference between being judged for one's physical beauty or lack of it and being considered unkempt and slightly scruffy, Sadie told herself. To be fair, she knew that the majority of employers in the financial sector preferred their employees to look smart and businesslike.

She reached down for her handbag, intending to open it and find a mirror to check to see if she looked as bad as she was beginning to feel, but before her fingers had curled round its handle Ali had materialised at her side, holding a tray on which she could see a full glass of pale, bubbling champagne and a plate of deliciously mouthwatering canapés. At the sight of her food her stomach gave a betraying rumble, which Ali effected not to notice.

'His Highness informed me that you may wish to use the guest suite. Please allow me to show you.' He had bent down and picked up her handbag before Sadie could stop him, leaving her with no real option other than to trot obediently alongside him as he guided her through the office-cum-lounge area into a narrow corridor that led to a pair of closed doors.

'This is the guest suite,' Ali told her, somehow managing to open the door while still carrying the tray and her handbag. 'The door next to it leads to the private suite of Their Highnesses. It is kept locked at all times, unless Their Highnesses specify otherwise.'

A subtle warning to her not to think of going snooping around to see what the Royal suite looked like? Sadie wondered as Ali held open the door for her to precede him into the guest suite.

To her amazement, it contained not only a large double bed but a wall of fitted cupboards and a built-in dressing table, plus two chairs and a small table. In the adjoining bathroom there was full-size shower and a basin.

Sadie looked at the shower. The thought of standing under it and washing the dust of Zuran off her hair and body was tempting— and not just because her skin felt so grubby and gritty from her hot walk. There would be something metaphorically beneficial about having a clean, fresh start to her life and her new job.

She would need a change of clothes, though. She had no idea where her case was, but as though he had read her mind Ali put the tray down on the table, placing her handbag beneath it, and then went to open the cupboard doors. Inside were her clothes, neatly hung up and looking undeniably tired and out of place in their luxurious new setting. A bit like her?

'Thank you, Ali,' she said to the hovering steward.

'You wish me perhaps to prepare the shower for you?' he asked politely.

'What? Oh, no...no. I can manage, thank you,' Sadie assured him swiftly.

It was silly of her to feel so overwhelmed. The Al Sawars had employed a large staff, and Monika's personal maid had done everything for her including running her bath. Sadie knew that.

Was it safe to have a shower now, while they were on the ground? she wondered. What would happen if they took off while she was in it? She had visions of water sloshing everywhere, ruining the carpets and perhaps even flooding into the forbidden Royal suite. She looked uncertainly at Ali.

'Is it all right to use the shower now?' she

asked him self-consciously. 'I mean, before we take off?'

'It is very good,' he assured her solemnly. 'The airplane, he does not go until His Highness is back on board. I will tell him that you use the shower and he will tell the Captain.'

If she was quick she might have time to be in and out of the shower and dressed before Drax returned. It would certainly give her pride a much-needed boost if she could present herself to him looking freshly groomed.

'Thank you, Ali,' she said to the steward again. 'I shall shower and change now, then, if that's all right?'

'It is very good,' Ali repeated. 'You will call me, please, if you wish anything? Perhaps more champagne?'

There was no lock on the bedroom door—but then there was no need for her to lock it, Sadie assured herself. She had never found the al Sawars' staff to be anything other than respectful and polite, and Ali certainly hadn't struck her as being anything other than trustworthy.

Five minutes later she stepped beneath the shower and felt the bliss of its warm water on

her skin, even better than she had anticipated.
To see the fine grains of sand sluicing down
with the water into the shower tray made her
change her mind about not bothering to wash
her hair. If she couldn't dry it then she would
plait it, and at least it would be clean—even if
it meant taking a longer shower than she had
planned.

Drax frowned as he watched the line of immaculately dressed young women handing over
the glossy designer logo carrier bags to his
waiting staff. He had bought what he had
thought most suitable—not just for a young
woman about to enter the employ of the ruling
house of Dhurahn, but also for the prospective
bride of one of them. Guessing Sadie's size for
the clothes hadn't been too much of a problem.
He had enough experience to make a pretty
shrewd estimate of her measurements. But to be
on the safe side he had instructed the boutiques
to supply the shoes they had suggested went
best with the outfits in two sizes. Now she would
have a wardrobe fit for a young woman well-
groomed enough to catch the eye of his fastidious brother, complete with some discreet
pieces of costume jewellery and a Cartier watch.

Drax stepped into the interior of the jet and the waiting stewards closed the doors.

'Where is Ms Murray?' he asked Ali as the steward offered him a glass of champagne, which he waved away.

'She asked me if there was sufficient time for her to take a shower before takeoff.'

Drax glanced at his watch.

She should be out of the shower by now. He got up and headed for the guest bedroom. He had no intention of warning Sadie of his plans for her, but he would have to give her some acceptable explanation for the new clothes he had bought her and make sure she wore them from now on.

Sadie was crouched on the floor, wrapped in a large bath towel, going through her almost empty suitcase with increasing disbelief and dismay, looking for the underwear that should have been there but so far she hadn't been able to find. She was oblivious to the brief knock on her door before Drax opened it and walked in.

The shock of seeing him brought her upright, but as she stood her foot caught in the trailing hem of the towel, causing it to slip from her body and leaving her completely naked.

For a heartbeat neither of them moved. Sadie couldn't even breathe, never mind retrieve the towel. But still her soft, pale-skinned rounded breasts lifted slightly, as though she had drawn in her breath, whilst her nipples, still damp from her shower and lightly gilded from the discreetly placed lighting, tightened subtly. But not so subtly that Drax's attention wasn't caught by their quick hardening—a hardening that was reciprocated far less subtly by his own body.

Without taking his gaze off her he pushed the door shut. Its soft click as it locked them together into the silent privacy of the bedroom made a small pulse jerk in Sadie's throat. She made a small sound, a protest that wasn't a protest at all, more a moan of female acknowledgement, her eyes widening as Drax took a step towards her.

It was almost as though she had been turned into two different people, Sadie thought. One of them, the Sadie she knew, was urging her frantically to pick up her towel and conceal her nakedness and her vulnerability with it. But the other Sadie, a Sadie who bemused and astonished her, wasn't listening. She was choosing to stay where she was; she felt only the pure female awareness of the power of her naked body and its right to accept the homage of the man who was subjecting its every curve and line with the look of a critic and a connoisseur.

Sadie had never stopped to think of her body as an object of artistic beauty before, and the Sadie she knew was horrified by the thought. But the other Sadie took pride in knowing that she could command the silent attention of such a man. *She* might as well have been a slave girl, commanded to stand before a man who would buy her for his pleasure, Sadie told herself, trying to goad this new, rebellious side of herself into submitting to angry shame. But instead *that* Sadie mocked her for her cowardice, and whispered to her that a slave girl could command the man who was her master if she had the courage to do so. She could give him such pleasure that *she* was the one who enslaved *him*—so that he was commanded by her pleasure to worship the sensuality she embodied. Such a woman knew how to tempt and torment a man until all he could think of was possessing her; until the slavery between them encompassed and held them both; until he was as shackled to her by the unseen chains of his own desire as surely as she was shackled in the market place for his inspection.

With every thought this unfamiliar Sadie had the old Sadie could feel herself becoming her, so that her belly hollowed erotically, and her breathing deepened and quickened, and the tight thrust of her nipples hardened into flushed arousal.

He had come here to tell her about the clothes he had bought for her, but the truth was, Drax decided, she didn't need clothes. She was perfect the way she was. And the heavy, unsteady thud of his heartbeat echoed the potency of his thoughts.

The only covering such perfection should have was that of his hands, exploring every silken centimetre of her soft flesh, or his lips, paying her the homage of his male hunger. She would taste of the fruits of her own country, ripe summer berries salted with just enough sharpness before being dipped in honey-sweetened cream that would meld on the tongue, leaving behind the memory of its velvet softness and warm scent. Her skin was as pale as the desert sand in the moonlight, her nipples the rose-gold of the dawn shadows on the mountains beyond the plain, the cleft between her legs as delicately hidden as one of the secret valleys deep in those mountains, concealed from the eyes of men.

If she were his he would command that she always came to him unclothed. He would build her a house with a secluded courtyard, its floor covered in the softest, deepest rugs, so that she could walk upon them without damaging the tender flesh of her feet. He would plant it with thornless roses and scented plants, so that when he took her in its seclusion the scent of the petals crushed beneath her body would release their perfume all around them. She would be his to enjoy as and when he wished.

But she wasn't going to be his. He had chosen her for his brother.

With one swift movement he reached down and retrieved her towel, handing it to her. His curt, 'Cover yourself,' brought Sadie out of the spell her unfamiliar half had woven around her, snapping her back to reality and to the humiliating embarrassment of her nudity.

She snatched the towel from Drax, holding in front of herself, her face on fire. 'You should have knocked,' she told him fiercely.

'I did. When you didn't answer I assumed... wrongly...' His eyes narrowed. 'Or perhaps the assumption I made was the right one? At least as far as *you* are concerned.'

It took several seconds for his meaning to reach her. When it did, the embarrassed pink of her face changed to an angry red.

'If you're trying to suggest that I *wanted* you to come in… Well, I didn't,' she told him flatly, when he didn't say anything. 'And now I'd like you to leave, please, whilst I get dressed.' It struck her that she was in no position to order him around on his own plane, but there was no way she was going to have him making those sort of accusations against her.

'You will have to be quick. I came to warn you that we are about to take off. You will need to be seated in the lounge area and wearing a seatbelt.'

'Fine. I'll only be two minutes.'

'You were looking for something when I came in?'

'It wasn't anything important,' Sadie said quickly. There was no way she could tell him that Monika's maid had omitted to pack her underwear in the case. And not just some of it. All of it.

'We can't waste any more time. There will be a robe in the bathroom—put that on.'

He obviously wasn't going to leave the bedroom without her, Sadie realised. She hesitated, and then, seeing the irritated look he was giving her, wrapped the towel tightly around herself and hurried into the bathroom to retrieve the robe she knew she ought to have put on in the first place.

While she was gone Drax looked at the bed. If he had followed his instincts right now she would be lying on it, her eyes closed in pleasure, her heart beating against the delicacy of her flesh, whilst he kissed and caressed her until she opened herself to him and begged him to possess her. But she wasn't his to possess. That pleasure would belong to Vere—if he chose to take it.

When Sadie emerged from the bathroom, securely wrapped in the bathrobe, Drax was standing beside the bedroom door—holding it open. His face was grim.

Was he going to tell her that he had changed his mind and there was no job for her after all? It frightened her to acknowledge how little she wanted to hear him say that.

CHAPTER FIVE

'CHAMPAGNE?' Drax asked curtly.

How decadent that would be—drinking champagne, dressed in a bathrobe, reclining in an expensive leather seat, in the company of a dangerously handsome and very wealthy man—and how completely opposite to her normal way of life.

'No, thank you,' Sadie said primly. She had already noticed the glossy carrier bags which seemed to fill almost half the floor space of the cabin, and her eyes darkened with an emotion she didn't want to admit to as she contemplated the woman they were destined for and her probable role in Drax's life. The role no doubt her unfamiliar self had been so busily and eagerly promoting for her!

Sadie could feel a hot wash of guilt burning through her body. Of *course* Drax would have a mistress. And more than one, to judge from the number of designer bags in the cabin. What did he do? Summon each one to spend the night with him in a strictly observed rota? Did they all live together, housed in opulent luxury in an old-fashioned-style seraglio, their beauty only ever seen by one man, the whole focus of their lives that of pleasing him and only him? What must that be like? To give oneself over totally and completely to one man's pleasure? To make it and him the whole purpose of one's life? To spend hour upon hour preparing your body for his possession in every way there was? She wasn't prepared for the fierce shudder that gripped her, convulsing her in a series of small physical pangs so intimate and betraying that they made her gasp softly in embarrassed shock.

Immediately Drax focused on her.

'You are afraid of flying?' he demanded sharply.

Well, that was one way of putting it, Sadie thought ruefully, but she shook her head. 'Afraid' wasn't exactly the way she would have described the emotion that had gripped her. Raging jealousy was closer to the mark.

Raging jealousy? Of the women in this man's harem? Had she gone completely mad?

'Then please fasten your seatbelt; we are about to take off.'

They certainly were. Almost before she had done as he'd instructed, she felt the power surge of the jet's engines as it raced down the runway and then lifted into the darkening blue of the early-evening sky. Below them Sadie could see the airport buildings, and then the city itself, and then they were banking and turning out into the Gulf itself, before soaring up into the starry sky.

'You can remove your seatbelt now. Ali will be serving us with a light meal shortly, but first there is something I want to discuss with you.'

This was it. He was going to tell her that he had changed his mind.

'It occurred to me that Monika might not only have retained your wages but also some of your personal possessions, including your clothes, and for that reason I have decided that it is both necessary and appropriate that a replacement wardrobe should be provided to you as part of your salary package. You will understand that, since you are to be working so closely with both myself and my brother on the preparatory work for our country's future as a new financial centre, your appearance must be commensurate with the status of this project. In my country a man is valued for what he is within himself, but nevertheless it is expected that his outer appearance is one that commands the respect of those around him. The poor beggar in the street will never be ignored or refused alms, but neither will he be invited to sit at the side of his ruler.

'I appreciate that in your own country it is not always considered acceptable for a male employer to provide a female employee with a new wardrobe, but here we live by different rules. Therefore, I hope you will understand and accept the necessity for me to provide you with clothing which I consider to be essential to your role.' She wouldn't, of course, grasp the hidden meaning within his words, Drax knew, since she had no idea what his real plans for her were.

'Are you saying that you're providing me with special working clothes?' Sadie queried uncertainly.

'Yes. Although the clothes I have acquired are yours to wear at all times—indeed, I wish to make it clear that you will be required to do so. It is important that you create the right impression even when you are not working.'

Sadie knew that clients in this part of the world could be very demanding, and very specific about their demands, and she was relieved that he was not telling her, as she had feared, that he had changed his mind.

'I expect the cost will be deducted from my salary, will it?' she asked him.

'No. That is not my intention. While we are having dinner Ali will take everything and pack it for you, but I shall require you to select one outfit to wear when we land and I introduce you to my brother. I would suggest the cream suit is probably a good choice.'

As he spoke Drax nodded his head in he direction of the massed carriers, causing Sadie to stare first at them and then at him, before demanding uncertainly, 'You aren't…? I mean, all those…? You can't mean that *all* those are for me!' But she could see from his expression that he did.

He gave a small dismissive shrug. 'We don't know how many formal events you will be called upon to attend. Naturally we shall require you to be appropriately dressed for every occasion.'

She couldn't believe this was happening—and neither could she remove her awed gaze from the glossy carrier bags as Ali served them the meal Drax had mentioned. Then, while Sadie ate food that wouldn't have been out of place in a Michelin-starred restaurant, Ali started to remove the bags to the bedroom.

'I've bought you a couple of cases to hold everything,' Drax told her. 'I appreciate that you won't want the embarrassment of arriving clutching an untidy array of carrier bags. My brother is an extremely fastidious man who prizes efficiency and neatness above all things.'

'I'll remember that,' Sadie answered dutifully, even as her mind went into overdrive. A designer-brand suit? She had never so much as possessed a designer lipstick, never mind a suit.

If any other man but this one had been offering her a designer wardrobe her suspicions would have been immediately aroused. But not only had Drax shown her that even if he wanted to have a physically intimate relationship with her he was ignoring it, she also knew from Monika that wealthy men here thought nothing of spending obscene amounts of money in ways that were not experienced at home. She had heard of employers handing out solid gold watches to employees for no better reason than that they felt like doing so, or ordering uniforms for their staff and then changing them on a whim because they had seen something else they liked better.

Even so... Sadie looked at the logos on the few remaining bags and swallowed. A cream suit wasn't going to be the only designer item in her new wardrobe. She just hoped that her new clothes were going to fit her.

As Sadie waited to descend the stairs from the now stationary jet, she smoothed the delicate silk skirt of the cream suit. It fitted her perfectly. And, from what she had seen of the rest of the new wardrobe she had been supplied with, the clothes were all in colours that were perfect for her—subtle creams and taupes, cool white linens, gorgeous chocolate-brown silks, and thankfully none of the prissy fussy pinks or patterns she had dreaded.

This suit, highlighted with gold thread and trimmed with antique lace, was simply cut, and yet had such a stunning elegance that it had her walking tall. She was glad she had taken the time to apply a little of the make-up she had found stacked with meticulous neatness into its own leather travelling case.

Her new luggage alone must have cost a small fortune, Sadie recognised. It was certainly far more exclusive than anything she could ever have afforded. She looked down at her strappy high-heeled shoes and wondered apprehensively if Drax's brother was going to approve of her being employed by him. She looked hesitantly at Drax, who was standing a few yards away from her, talking to the Captain of the jet.

So far he hadn't said a word about her transformed appearance, or the suit—though he had flicked an assessing glance over her when she'd stepped uncertainly into the main cabin, having changed into her new clothes. Did that mean that he was satisfied with her appearance or that he wasn't? She wasn't going to admit to herself that his lack of response had disappointed her. He was her employer, nothing more, and there was no reason why he should comment and no reason why she should wish him to do so.

'Ready?'

She had been so busy refusing to admit to wanting his approval that she hadn't noticed that he had stopped talking to the Captain and was now coming over to her.

'Yes. I... I put on the cream suit, as you suggested. I hope your brother...'

'It looks fine.'

She was wearing her hair up, and several fine tendrils had escaped from the knot at the nape of her neck and were starting to curl softly round her face. The silk stroked lovingly against her body, hinting sensuously at what it concealed as though it were a lover. The fabric itself possessed a quality that made him want to reach out and touch it—and her. He had been aware of that need from the moment she had stepped into the cabin, looking at him with eyes that held both uncertainty and a shy appeal. For what? For him to tell her that she was a highly desirable woman? He couldn't do that. But he wanted to do it. He wanted to tell her to show her just how sexy he found her.

No! He had chosen her for Vere. But that suit was perhaps not the best choice for his brother to see her for the first time. Its soft sensuality underlined her own equally soft sensuality, and would not appeal to Vere. He should have chosen something more tailored, more conservative, Drax told himself as he waited for Ali to open the cabin door.

* * *

'When you said you'd bought some luggage for the clothes, I didn't realise…that is…'

They were in the back of a leather-upholstered Bentley, being driven to the palace down a wide straight road, with the sea on one side and the lights of Dhurahn city on the other. The road was lined with palm trees, their trunks decorated with tiny fairy lights, and the overhead street lighting revealed immaculate flowerbeds set into green verges. Theirs wasn't the only car on the road, but the Royal pennant fluttering from the bonnet ensured that other traffic gave way so their progress was speedy and stately.

Drax had hardly spoken to her since they had landed, and she still wasn't over the shock of seeing over half a dozen brand-new cream leather suitcases being loaded into the car and realising they contained her new clothes.

'I've already explained the situation with regard to my decision to provide you with a new wardrobe. The matter is now closed.'

Drax didn't even look at her as he spoke, and it was obvious to Sadie that he did not wish to engage in conversation with her, but nevertheless there were questions she needed to ask him.

'We haven't discussed where I am to stay

while I am working for you. If it is to be a government-owned apartment, will the rent—?'

'You will be staying in the palace and there will be no rent.'

'In the palace? You mean with you?' The moment the words had left her lips Sadie realised how gauche they sounded, and wished she could recall them, but it was too late. Drax was turning to look at her. In the dark interior of the car his face was highlighted by the streetlights so that she could see its aquiline arrogance. Sadie felt a fierce need to reach out and trace the harshly etched strength. His skin would feel warm beneath her fingertips, the savagely sensual shape of his mouth smooth to her touch…

'I mean that you will be accommodated in the women's quarters within the palace complex.'

'The women's quarters? You mean I'll be staying in a harem?'

Was she imagining that the green gaze had ignited with dark fire?

'The men of my family have for many generations been monogamous and faithful to their single chosen wife. It might excite your imagination to believe otherwise, but that is not the case. There is no harem as such within the walls of the palace. Nevertheless, we are a free society here in Dhurahn. Our people can worship as they please, and we are bound to respect their religious beliefs. Thus we adhere to the tradition of maintaining a separate women's quarter within the palace complex. Our visiting female guests feel more comfortable knowing that their traditions will be respected.'

'But I am not a guest. I am an employee—'

'You have worked in Zuran, so you will be aware that the Ruler there conducts administrative business from within the palace, which is also his private residence and that of his extended family. It is the same for us here in Dhurahn. The palace is our home, but it is also the centre from which our country is run. Members of our extended family as well as some senior officials and their families live and work in the palace. There will be nothing untoward in you residing within the complex. In fact it might be considered rather unusual if you did not. Here, there is normally only one reason a man sets a woman up in her own apartment—and, though it might be a business arrangement, I do not think it is one you would wish to be associated with.'

Sadie's face had begun to burn as she listened to him. He had managed to make her feel both naïve and ignorant of the region's customs.

While they had been talking the car had slowed to a halt outside a pair of huge, beautifully decorated wrought-iron gates depicting a pair of peacocks, their tails spread and studded with richly coloured stones—not *real* jewels? Sadie wondered faintly as the gates swung open and the uniformed guards beyond saluted and then salaamed.

Inside the gates there was a large courtyard, beyond which a flight of cream marble steps led up to a columned portico and a pair of tall wooden doors.

The moment the car stopped alongside the steps the wooden doors opened and a line of household staff appeared, all of them wearing the same livery.

It was like stepping into something out of history, Sadie decided. The kind of gilded luxury she had never imagined experiencing. It should have at worst appalled her and at best overwhelmed her, but as she stood next to

Drax, listening to him greeting each man in turn and seeing the way they smiled back at him, she recognised that she was witnessing genuine respect and affection between the co-Ruler of Dhurahn and those who served him.

'My brother?' Sadie heard Drax ask.

'Highness, His Highness sends his apologies for not being here to welcome you home. He is in his private rooms and has asked that you go to him there as soon as you are able.'

Drax frowned. It would be a grave breach of court protocol for him to take Sadie to Vere's private rooms, and he was disappointed that Vere wasn't here to greet them so he could see his brother's amazement when he saw her.

'Please take Ms Murray to the women's quarters and see that she is made comfortable while I speak with my brother,' he instructed one of the waiting men, before turning to Sadie. She looked calm and at ease, her manner towards the palace staff as she inclined her head and smiled both warm and yet just distant enough to command respect. Vere would appreciate that in her, Drax approved, and he went to her and touched her lightly on her arm.

Sadie was amazed at how intensely she

could feel the virile warmth of Drax's touch through the soft fabric of her jacket. It jerked her out of the tiredness that had come to seep through her and made her whole body stiffen slightly.

'I have to go and see my brother. Nasim will escort you to the women's quarters. They will make you comfortable there. Please feel free to ask for anything you might need. '

He was turning away from her before she could respond, taking the long flight of marble stairs that led upward to a balcony enclosed by fretted shutters that could conceal anyone watching from above. As she looked upwards Sadie gave a small shudder, suddenly feeling very alone and very alien, as though she were in fact being studied by unseen watchers hidden away from her view.

'This way, please, lady.' Nasim bowed low to her before guiding her towards a door that led off the hallway.

It was foolish in the extreme for her to wish that Drax had not left her, to wish that she could run after him and beg him to stay with her. Foolish and very dangerous—she was going to pretend she hadn't thought it.

* * *

'Drax. I have missed you.'

'I have been gone less than a week.' Drax smiled as he and Vere embraced.

'The palace seems quiet when you are gone, my brother,' Vere told him ruefully. 'I am sorry I was not able to welcome you back, but I am preparing to leave for London now. My main meeting has been brought forward, and at this stage in the negotiations I didn't feel that I could object.

'I was disappointed not to see your reaction to the bride I have found you.'

'I saw her in the hallway.'

'Yes,' Drax agreed, his suspicion that his brother had been looking down on them confirmed. 'She is most suitable for our purpose, Vere. Educated, intelligent enough to be groomed as your bride, of good moral character, and naïve too; you only have to persuade her to fall in love with you, and—'

'She is neither blonde enough nor tall enough for my taste, Drax. You know I prefer the cool elegance of a soignée blonde.'

'You will be marrying her, Vere. Not taking her to bed.'

'If I am to persuade her to fall in love with me surely there will come a time when I shall be obliged to at least initiate *some* intimacy between us?'

Drax could sense that Vere was watching him very closely, but it still stunned him when Vere suggested quietly, 'Perhaps you should think of marrying her yourself?'

'No. I brought her here for you. I promised I would find you a wife first. We can discuss it further on your return. Is there anything you need me to brief you on before you leave for London?'

'You mentioned Sir Edward Reeves and his opposition to our proposals. You said that you thought the best way to handle that would be via a personal meeting with him?'

'Yes. I spoke to his people whilst I was in London, and I've set things in motion for you to meet with him. He's one of the old school of diplomats. He fears that a financial exchange here might not operate with the probity he considers necessary.'

'I shall endeavour to convince him otherwise. And now I must go.'

'I'll walk you to your car.'

'To persuade me to reconsider the charms of Ms Murray?' Vere asked lightly.

'No. When you return, you will witness

them for yourself—and then you will need no persuading,' Drax told him suavely.

Sadie was so tired she was almost falling asleep sitting upright on the slightly uncomfortable low chair—obviously designed for women who were more used to sitting elegantly cross-legged.

Nasim had handed her over to a plump, smiling woman wearing a feminine version of his own livery. She had introduced herself as Alama and then shown her into a large, luxuriously carpeted and furnished salon before disappearing. Several minutes later a shy young girl who'd introduced herself as Hakeem had appeared, to ask her in uncertain English if she would like coffee. Sadie had refused, knowing that drinking the strong local coffee would keep her awake. Now, though, she was beginning to regret her refusal, and longed for a drink of water.

How long would she have to stay here for? Until she was summoned before Drax and his brother to be inspected?

The door to the salon opened and Alama came in, accompanied by Nasim.

'His Highness wishes to speak with you,'

Alama informed her. 'Nasim will escort you to him, and then, when you return, Hakeem will be waiting for you, to take you to your rooms.'

Nasim escorted her back down the passageway he had brought her along earlier, taking her through the hallway and into a room off it that was obviously some kind of office. Drax was there, seated behind a large desk, frowning as he studied a computer screen.

'Regrettably, my brother has had to leave without meeting you,' he told her as he waved her into the chair opposite his own. 'It will be several days before he returns from London, and during that time...'

Sadie could hardly believe what she was hearing. She was tired, and her head was aching. In the last twenty-four hours she had lost one job, been denied her rightful wages and then been virtually thrown out in the street. She had been bemused, bullied and virtually blackmailed into accepting a job in another country, and then told that it was necessary for her to dress in designer label clothes in order to gain the approval of a man who now apparently had disappeared and was not likely to return any time soon. That was if he had ever existed in the first place.

She had, she decided, had enough. In fact, she had had *more* than enough! She pushed back her chair and stood up, then drew herself up to her full height and told Drax fiercely, 'During that time I shall have returned to London. You virtually kidnapped me, and then blackmailed me into coming here with you. You said that you had a job for me, and that your reasons for wanting to bring me were are all completely above board. Then you demanded that I wear clothes that you bought for me so I would gain the approval of your brother—even though when you offered me the job you didn't mention his approval was necessary. And now you tell me that this brother of yours isn't here. Well, do you know what I think?' Sadie challenged him angrily. 'I think that this brother of yours and the job you've offered me have a great deal in common. In that neither of them has any existence outside your imagination.'

She shook her head bitterly. 'It's my own fault, I know. I made it all so easy for you, didn't I? You'd have thought that after what I'd experienced with Monika al Sawar I'd have had more sense than to believe you.'

While she had been talking, letting her wild angry words tumble hotly into the silence, Drax's expression had undergone a subtle change which, now that he too was pushing back his chair and standing up, made him look every inch the kind of haughty, autocratic male who held the power of life and death over those he ruled. But it was too late to wish she had been more circumspect—and besides, why *shouldn't* she tell him what she thought?

'If you are trying to say that you believe I have *lied* to you—'

'I'm not *trying* to say that. I *am* saying it,' Sadie said, standing her ground. And then felt her knees tremble when he let out his breath in a hiss of suppressed fury.

'There is no job, is there? Just like there is no brother,' she challenged him. 'And you have brought me here—'

'For what purpose?' Drax stopped her even while he reflected inwardly that it was just as well Vere wasn't here to witness her outburst. Vere was emotionally controlled, often remote, and very much aware of his position and what was owed to him. Sadie's emotional fury would only have added to his brother's conviction that she was not a suitable candidate to become his temporary wife. Sadie, on the other hand, obviously thought it was a very different role Drax had in mind for her.

When she didn't answer him, but instead compressed her mouth and gave a mute shake of her head, he spoke softly, deliberately spacing out each and every word. 'I thought I had already made it clear to you that I have no sexual interest in you. It is well known that there is a certain type of over-excitable foreign woman who seems to assume that men of my country are unable to resist her charms. It is a subject of some amusement for us.' He gave a small dismissive shrug. 'One sees it in their eyes. There is hunger and stupidity... It takes no great intelligence to know that such women come here already fantasising about having sex with a robed lover.'

He gave another shrug. 'There are, of course, some young men who amuse themselves by encouraging these women's fantasies while laughing at them when their backs are turned. It occurs to me that in repeatedly accusing me of having sexual designs on you, you may be concealing your own sexual curiosity.'

Sadie gasped in outrage. 'That is not true! There is only one reason I came here with you. And that is because you virtually forced me.'

'I offered you a job, which you accepted.'

'Because you virtually blackmailed me into it! You refused to return my passport, and you still have it.'

'Indeed I do, and I intend to keep it until you have completed the probationary period we agreed on. And let me warn you—this is the second time you have made the kind of accusations against me that no man bears unpunished. Just remember that, if you should be tempted to repeat them a third time. My brother, as I said, has been called away on urgent business. However, I have spoken of you to him, and he agrees with me that you will be perfect for the position we have in mind.'

It was the truth, after all—even if Vere had rejected her and proposed that Drax should be the one to have her. He was almost tempted to take on the challenge and tame the wild cat she had just proved herself to be—in his bed, where he would make sure she purred with pleasure for him instead of hissing and spitting as she was doing now. She had certainly angered and aroused him enough for him to want to punish her for her audacity. There was unexpected spice beneath the outer meek blandness of her manner, Drax acknowledged, and, having exposed it, like any man worthy of the name he naturally wanted to explore it. And to conquer it, and her?

Drax mentally shrugged aside the sly thought that had somehow insinuated itself into his mind. He could find himself the necessary temporary wife easily enough, but Vere was not like him. Vere had a tendency to withdraw and hold himself aloof, which meant that he did not always find it easy to forge relationships with those outside the rarefied atmosphere in which they lived. The truth was that the kind of arranged inter-Royal family marriage their fellow rulers were proposing for them was probably the kind that *would* best suit his brother—although Vere himself was not likely to admit to that, Drax knew. Neither of them liked having his hand forced—they both had a fierce determination to be masters of their own fate—but Vere, once he had set his mind to something, could not be swayed and would not compromise.

He had said that he did not want to be inveigled into a diplomatic marriage, and that suited *him,* Drax admitted, because at the moment he did not want to marry full-stop. While he knew that his way of life and his method of doing things seemed unorthodox, compared to Vere's rigid adherence to protocol, Drax had his own strong sense of where his loyalties lay and how he felt about them.

For all that Vere was the firstborn, and carried about a certain sternness and an air of discipline, as if it was his duty to take on board more of the sometimes onerous weight of their shared responsibility, Drax often felt as though he was the more senior. He was the one who was more in touch with the realities of modern life and who had lived out in the world. He also knew that sometimes he protected his brother. But it was, to Drax, part of what their twinship meant that he should give this service of care to his brother without remarking on it.

In deciding that Sadie would make an ideal temporary wife for Vere, Drax had been doing what he had done all his life—he had seen Vere's need and potential vulnerability and had stepped in to ensure that his brother was protected. He did not want to acknowledge, never mind accept, that there was something about Sadie that was making him physically aware of her—and not just aware, but hungry for her. Sadie was merely a woman who fitted a specific purpose, and she would be adequately recompensed once it came to an end. As far as Drax was concerned there was very little difference in paying off a no longer wanted mistress and a no longer wanted temporary wife. Both should be removed from one's life with speed and efficiency and the minimum of fuss. Other men might indulge in the folly of 'falling in love', but Drax knew that he would never allow that to happen to him.

Their parents' death, especially the loss of their mother, had left both Vere and Drax exposed to the old-fashioned mindset of their father's well-meaning but rather traditional royal advisers. With no women playing a prominent role in the country's government over the past decade, they had been encouraged to develop a somewhat dismissive attitude towards romantic love.

Drax flicked another assessing look over Sadie, frowning as he saw her trying to smother a tell-tale yawn.

'It has been a long day for you, and it is late. I shall summon Nasim and instruct him to escort you back to the women's quarters. Tomorrow will be time enough for me to discuss my plans for our new venture with you in more detail.'

CHAPTER SIX

SADIE came up through the heavy layers of her deep sleep slowly and reluctantly on hearing the soft sounds of padding feet and the chink of china. When she opened her eyes it confused her at first not to see the bare discomfort of her small room high up under the roof of the al Sawar house.

And then she remembered. She wasn't in Zuran any more; she was in the Royal Palace of Dhurahn.

She sat up quickly in the comfortable wide bed, thankful that she had taken the trouble to slip on a clean tee shirt before going to bed. Was that because she had feared that her sleep might be interrupted not by the shyly smiling Hakeem, who had just brought her a breakfast tray, but by the man who had brought her here?

Drax. Prince al Drac'ar al Karim bin Hakar. Just thinking about him was enough not only to raise the heat of her body, but to make her sensually aware of the cool stroke of the undoubtedly expensive bedlinen against her suddenly sensitised skin. She could feel the pulse of her own body, and the ache it sent radiated out all over her, making her nipples tighten and her toes want to curl.

She must not think like this, Sadie warned herself, shocked by the waywardness of her thoughts. She made herself focus on Hakeem, who was telling her softly, 'I have brought you your breakfast, *sheikha*. If there is anything else you should wish?'

Sheikha? Surely she had no right to such an elevated form of address? Or was the girl simply being polite? It frustrated Sadie that her knowledge of Dhurahni customs was so limited. That was sómething she would have to address if she was to stay and work here.

Her thoughts suddenly busy, Sadie refused to admit to herself that she might be keeping them that way to resist giving in to the temptation of thinking about her new employer.

She smiled at the waiting girl and shook her head. 'No. This is lovely. Thank you.'

'I am to return in one hour to escort you to the public rooms of the palace, where you will be met by of one His Highness's assistants,' she told Sadie carefully, as though she had been rehearsing the words.

Sadie gave her another smile. She was glad she'd have someone to show her the way along the corridors. She had been too tired to take much note when she was whisked down them last night.

With Hakeem gone, Sadie got out of bed, tempted by the shafts of sunlight coming in through the open shutters of the windows to see what lay outside them. She had also been too tired to explore the suite of rooms she had been given, but this morning she could see just how luxurious her bedroom was. Its décor was an eye-pleasing mixture of traditional and modern. The bed was wide and low, a beautiful silk rug hung on the wall opposite the bed, and several more equally beautiful rugs were scattered over the tiled floor. Two sets of double doors opened off the bedroom on opposite walls adjacent to the windows. One set led into an elegantly furnished sitting room-cum-office, and the other into a wardrobe-lined dressing room which opened up into a large, modern bathroom with limestone floors and a huge free-standing 'infinity' bath.

Pulling on the towelling robe she had left at the end of the bed the night before, Sadie went over to the windows. As she looked out her eyes widened in delight when she saw the enclosed courtyard garden that lay beyond them. A pair of French windows opened out onto a tiled area, protected from the sunlight by a deep veranda. Beyond that were mosaic pathways and raised flowerbeds filled with a variety of hosta-like wide-leaved plants and neatly clipped topiary balls of white roses. The beds were finished off with a border of frothing white flowers Sadie didn't recognise. In the middle of the enclosed area water splashed down from a fountain into a basin which overflowed into an ornamental stone-edged pond. As she watched, a large, sleek, beautifully-coloured fish rose from the water to snap at a hovering fly before subsiding back into the water.

Even from inside the room Sadie could smell the scent of the roses. Beyond the enclosed area was a miraculously green hedge, no doubt watered by some under-soil watering system. In the hedge was a 'doorway', which led to yet another garden—this one, so far as she could see from the window, containing more roses and topiary.

Sadie had never ever stayed anywhere so luxurious—made all the more sensual because it was so discreetly understated. She picked up the cup of coffee Hakeem had poured for her and drank it quickly. It was hot and sweet, although a bit strong for her taste. There was also a basket filled with small, sweet, sticky pastries, a selection of fruit and a bottle of water. But Sadie wasn't hungry. In fact her stomach had started to churn with apprehension as she remembered the interview she'd had with Drax the previous evening.

Telling herself that it wouldn't be a good idea to be late for her meeting with him, she poured herself another cup of coffee and drank it quickly, before hurrying into the bathroom.

Now, *this* was the kind of luxury she could easily get used to, she admitted as she paused to admire the infinity bath. There was no time for lingering this morning, though. A shower would be quicker, and probably far more therapeutic as it wouldn't encourage her to indulge in thinking about Drax.

Half an hour later she was ready—her hair washed, blown dry and neatly secured, her body clothed in what seemed to be the plainest of her new clothes—a neutral-coloured linen-mix skirt with a white short-sleeved, softly fitting top embellished with decorative natural-coloured 'stone' buttons at the shoulders and on the small V-shaped neckline. His Highness, it seemed, had thought of everything—including, as she had just discovered, two pairs of designer sunglasses.

She had no idea what on earth she would do with all these things when she returned to the UK. She certainly hoped he didn't expect her to want to keep them and then pay for them out of her wages. She would be paying for them for the rest of her working life, judging by the labels. But then perhaps to a man as obviously wealthy as Drax the cost of supplying an employee with a wardrobe bulging with designer labels was an insignificant perk. And the clothes weren't for her; they were for an employee. She was a visual attachment to a very important venture, and as such she had to project the right image.

Sadie could hear the outer door of her suite opening. It was Hakeem, coming to collect her. Quickly slipping her feet into a pair of pretty shell-decorated summer mules, she hurried out of the dressing room, smiling at the young girl patiently waiting for her.

'Heavens, I'll never get used to all these corridors,' she told Hakeem ten minutes later, envying the other 'girl's elegant, straight-backed walk as she led her down a series of interconnecting white-walled corridors. She would have loved to have had time to stop and study the paintings and artwork, with their rich, vivid colours and sculptured lines, but Hakeem obviously didn't want to linger. Like the domestic staff employed by the wealthy in Zuran, Hakeem was Indian, and so delicately beautiful that Sadie felt clumsy and awkward beside her despite her new clothes.

'It was kind of you to bring me my breakfast this morning, Hakeem,' Sadie said, and thanked her.

'You like?' Hakeem gave her another shy smile. 'And you like the bedroom of the Royal Princesses? It is very beautiful, is it not?' she asked proudly. 'We have had only the ladies of the Royal Household of Zuran to stay in it before, when the Sheikha, who was the mother of our Rulers, was alive. But that was a long time ago—before I was here. It was before I was here too that Their Highnesses' mother and father were killed and the whole of

Dhurahn mourned their loss. It was very sad for such a dreadful thing to happen.'

'Their parents were killed?'

'It was in a car,' Hakeem told her solemnly. 'But not here,' she assured Sadie hastily. 'And it was a long time ago.'

'How dreadful.' Sadie couldn't help shivering a little as she contemplated how awful it must have been for Drax and Vere to learn that such a terrible thing had happened to both their parents.

'It was very sad,' Hakeem repeated. 'Everyone loved the Sheikha, even though she was not Dhurahni and, like you, came from a land far away. Ireland.'

Another time it would have made Sadie smile gently to see how carefully Hakeem pronounced the unfamiliar word. But how could she smile when she had just heard about such a tragedy?

'It is unusual to hear of a Dhurahni prince marrying a European girl,' she told Hakeem, guessing that she was expected to make some comment on her story.

'Not so here. Here it is tradition,' Hakeem corrected her firmly.

Before Sadie could question her any further,

she indicated a pair of heavily carved dark, polished doors in front of them, and said, 'Ahmed will be waiting for you outside the doors to the women's quarters to escort you to His Highness, *sheikha.*' She then salaamed gracefully and backed away from Sadie.

'Hakeem—' Sadie began, about to question the maid's manner of addressing her. But it was too late. The double doors were opening and Ahmed was now salaaming to her.

He led her not back to the room, where she had seen Drax last night, but down a corridor and then through a large room ornately decorated, its furniture heavily gilded and its low sofas piled high with richly jewelled silk cushions.

At one end there was a raised dais with two throne-like chairs on it, and Sadie guessed that the room must be the audience chamber where the brothers held their formal *divan*—the event at which any subject could present his petition to his rulers and be heard.

However, they still had to negotiate another long corridor before finally Ahmed led her across a square hallway so plain in its architectural design and furnishings that the contrast between it and the rooms she had just seen was like receiving a glass of cold pure water after the stickiness of spiced wine.

The floor of the hallway was tiled with matt black tiles. A stairway led to an upper gallery, its banister carved out of some ebony-coloured wood, the symmetry of its curves so perfect and plain that it made Sadie catch her breath.

After knocking briefly on the closed double doors, and then opening them for her, indicating that she was to step through, Ahmed salaamed again and then backed away.

A little hesitantly, Sadie walked through the doors. The room beyond them was as modern and breathtaking as the hallway, and three times the size. It was a combination of a living area and an office, its furniture made from the same dark wood as the stairs, the seating streamlined and stylish.

A huge plate glass window looked out onto a courtyard, enclosed on three sides by the modern architecture of the building, with a large swimming pool at the far end.

Awed, she stared at the pool—and then realised it was occupied. Her heart thumped heavily into her ribs as she watched Drax place his hands on the walkway, his flesh hard and tanned, the water running off his shoulders and chest, and spring lithely out of the water, completely naked, before turning his back towards her as he reached for the robe on a recliner. Her heart was racing so frantically she had to breathe faster to keep up with it. *Had* he been naked? Or had she just thought that he was? Had that brief glimpse of male nudity before he turned his back on her been the product of her imagination? Surely he wouldn't have swum naked knowing that he might be seen? Why not? an inner voice challenged her. He was one of the ruling Princes of a rich Arab kingdom, and so arrogant that he probably did exactly what he felt like when he felt like it. Who was there to stop or question him after all?

He had disappeared out of sight, but her heartbeat still hadn't returned to normal.

'You were admiring the view?'

The sound of his voice behind her had her swinging around, her face burning. While she had been staring out into the courtyard like an awestruck virgin, he had entered the room and was now walking towards her, still wearing his robe and making a very subtle and mocking reference to the fact that she had seen him getting out of the pool.

Well, two could play at that game, Sadie decided angrily.

'It's a very clever effect,' she answered him coolly. 'Very pared down and sparse. I like the clean lines and the sense of space—although of course we all know that it is merely a trick of the design that makes less look more.'

She was quick—and clever, Drax acknowledged. He had embarrassed her, he knew that, but she still had the wit to parry words with him. But how long would she be able to keep it up? Drax decided to put her to the test.

'And, like most of your sex, you always opt for *more*—is that it?'

She was getting into deep water now, Sadie admitted uncomfortably, all too aware of the double meaning behind the mocking words.

'It surprised me to see such modern architecture…' She had meant to bring the subtle *double entendre* element to their conversation to an end with her reply, but when she saw the way he was looking at her, her expression gave her away. 'I mean, all of this…' she amended hastily, waving her hand in the direction of the entire room. 'It is lovely but…not what I expected.'

'So that is twice this morning you have

witnessed something you weren't expecting, then?'

Sadie opened her mouth and then closed it again. Her whole body was burning now.

'Such embarrassment—and all over a glimpse of a naked male body,' he taunted her softly. 'You surprise me, Sadie. I had thought you would be rather more sophisticated.' He gave a dismissive shrug. 'I'm sorry if you were embarrassed, but I didn't realise Ahmed had shown you in here until it was too late.'

Inwardly Drax was thinking that Vere would be pleased that she was so easily embarrassed. It pointed to a genuine lack of experience that would please his fastidious brother. As it pleased *him?* He frowned. Why should *he* have any personal opinions on the matter of her experience or lack of it?

'He did knock on the door.' Sadie didn't want him thinking she had come in of her own accord, or that she had *wanted* to catch sight of him levering himself out of the pool.

Drax gave another small shrug. 'It isn't important. As I've already said, I'm sorry you were embarrassed. Now, I shall ring for Ahmed to bring you some coffee, and I'll go and get dressed. I want to show you the building we intend to use as the headquarters for our new financial sector. We've put aside a hundred acres of land which will be used exclusively to house the financial business sector. The main building has already been constructed and is finished, ready for use.' And, as Vere had already said, they would be left with it on their hands if their meetings failed and they did not get approval to go ahead.

Although Drax was covered from his throat to below his knees by his robe, Sadie was acutely aware that beneath it he was naked—and male. Very male indeed, if her brief glimpse of him had been accurate. Not that she had seen enough nude men in the flesh to compare. But it had been obvious to her that Drax was boldly 'endowed', as the saying went.

Drax knew that he was embarrassing her, Sadie recognised.

'I hadn't expected that the palace would look so modern,' she confessed, determined to change the subject before it got too out of hand.

Was he actually giving her a small smile—too mocking and knowing for her peace of mind—or was she just imagining it?

'Not all of it does. Only this new wing, which I have had added as my own private quarters. My brother is a traditionalist at heart, and he prefers the design and décor of our forebears. He did not altogether approve initially when I told him what I planned to do.'

'But it looks wonderful,' Sadie assured him quickly, and then, worried that she might have sounded horribly sycophantic, added lamely, 'I've always preferred modern architecture and design.'

'It has its benefits,' Drax agreed.

For some reason she was thinking about the swimming pool and his naked body again, Sadie realised guiltily, and rushed to ask, 'As I won't be meeting your brother, presumably I don't have to wear the Chanel suit today?'

'Not whilst you are alone with me, no,' Drax allowed.

What was it about those words 'alone' and 'with me' that set her heart rocketing into her chest wall? Did she really need to ask herself that question? Wasn't the answer openly obvious in the way her body was reacting? And did that small smile Drax was giving her mean that he had guessed what she was thinking? Oh, please not, Sadie prayed inwardly. The last thing she wanted was for this arrogant and sexually potent man to know that she had unconsciously filed the mental image she had of his powerful male physique to review again when she was on her own. Heavens, it shocked her enough to have to admit to *herself* what she had done, never mind have him know about it as well.

'However,' Drax continued, forcing her to abandon her frantic inner thoughts and listen, 'Dhurahn is a very small state. It will soon become common knowledge why you are here. There are already several independent European financial services people resident in Dhurahn city. They refer to themselves as entrepreneurs —although I am aware that the financial press often prefer to refer to them as predators.'

'You invited them here?' Sadie asked.

'No, they are not here at our invitation. These are not the sort of people we would want.' His mouth curled in disdainful dislike. 'They are vultures. Like all their kind, they possess an early-warning system that alerts them to the scent of fresh blood. However, you may rest assured that they will not be allowed to get rich on the backs of citizens of this country. I must warn you that everything that is discussed between us is privileged and confidential information, and must remain as such.'

'Are you saying that my contract of employment will contain penalty clauses for breach of confidence?'

Drax eyed her thoughtfully. She had, of course, no idea what her ultimate 'employment' was going to be, nor how apt her question was. Certainly when Vere married her she would be signing a pre-nuptial agreement. It was a great pity that Vere couldn't see her now. The top she was wearing hinted at the softness of her breasts, her skin showed the beginnings of a faint tan, and Drax was pleased to see that she was wearing only minimal make-up. It had amused him earlier to see the shocked expression on her face when he had leapt naked out of the pool, but his amusement had rebounded on him when his body had reacted to the knowledge that she was watching him. He had had to turn his back on her very quickly to conceal his reaction from her. He should not, of course, have allowed such a situation to arise at all. *Arise* being the operative word, he admitted grimly. Because he certainly had been aroused. Extremely aroused. So much so that even now...

She was going to marry his brother, he reminded himself. He was determined about that. So determined that he had already given the household a subtle indication of her future role as a Royal wife by installing her in the Royal suite of the women's quarters.

'Your quarters are satisfactory?' he asked her now, remembering his duties as a host. 'You have everything you need?'

'The suite is magnificent,' Sadie answered him truthfully. 'But…'

'But?' Drax demanded.

'Hakeem, the little maid, keeps addressing me as *sheikha,* even though I have tried to tell her that I do not hold such a title.'

Drax tensed momentarily. It would not do for Sadie to get wind of what he was planning before she had had the chance to meet Vere and he had put his plan into action by encouraging her to fall for him.

He gave a deliberately dismissive shrug. 'It is merely a formal mode of address. She no doubt means simply to be polite to you. However, if you would rather have someone else to attend you…?'

'No…no. She is lovely. She…she has been telling me about the palace and your family, and—' Sadie could see him tensing and stopped, but it was too late.

'And?' he probed.

'She also told me about your parents,' Sadie admitted, adding quietly, 'What a dreadful thing to have happened.'

'Yes, it was.' Drax's answer was so terse that Sadie wished she hadn't said anything. Had she inadvertently touched a still raw wound? Didn't it make sense that the loss of one's parents in such a horrific accident would *always* leave a raw wound?

She had been tactless, she decided guiltily. 'I'm sorry. I shouldn't have mentioned it.'

Both her guilt and her apology were so genuine that they made Drax frown. He wasn't used to people treating him as though he was vulnerable and could be emotionally hurt. To be aware of her compassion touched a nerve within him that produced the echo of an old and deep pain.

'My mother didn't have to go that day. But she always went everywhere with my father. Theirs was a true love match. She used to say that I had inherited personality traits from her side of the family—she was Irish.'

'Yes, Hakeem told me. That explains why

you have green eyes, of course—' Sadie stopped speaking abruptly, and put her hand to her lips in consternation.

'Yes, Vere and I share her eyes. But Vere inherited the preferences of our paternal ancestors. It is traditional for scholarly men to take an interest in our literature and to write classical poetry; it is as much a part of being a Dhurahni prince as is the love of falconry and the desert, and Vere has already won renown for his skill in the writing of poetic verse. I, on the other hand, while I too love the desert and honour our traditions, have inherited my mother's grandfather's love of architecture and design. Our parents valued both aspects of our dual inheritance because they reflected what they each saw and loved in each other.'

What was happening to him? Drax challenged himself angrily. He couldn't believe he had just spoken so intimately to Sadie. He never talked about his parents to anyone other than Vere. He comforted himself that at least their conversation had given him an opportunity to bring Vere's virtues to her attention. If his brother wasn't here to encourage Sadie to fall in love with him then he would just have to do his best to help her to do so in his absence. The fact that earlier she had aroused him meant nothing, less than nothing, he assured himself, and if it did happen again... If it did? It wouldn't. He intended to make sure of that.

'To lose them both must have been unbearable,' he could hear Sadie saying.

Was she right in thinking that his words of praise for his brother masked an unacknowledged feeling that his brother had been their parents' favourite because he was the elder son? Sadie wondered compassionately. If so, how foolish of his parents not to value him as he so obviously deserved to be valued.

Sadie felt angrily protective on his behalf. Was the arrogance she had seen in him simply a means of protecting himself? Like these rooms, pared down and clinically bare of any softening personal things? Her compassion for him grew, startling her when she realised that it was making her feel almost tenderly protective of him. What on earth was happening to her? He was her employer. That was all. She had no need to feel protective of him and he was hardly likely to want it.

Without Vere, the loss of their parents would have been unbearable, Drax admitted to himself. But he had no intention of telling Sadie that. Instead, he said distantly, 'It had to be borne. That was our duty to Dhurahn and to them.'

His cold sharpness speedily dissipated Sadie's compassionate concern. She was a fool to feel sorry for him—a fool to feel *anything* for him, she warned herself firmly, as Ahmed arrived with the coffee.

To Sadie's relief, if the manservant thought it oddly intimate that his master should be talking to his new employee dressed only in a towelling robe he was too tactful to betray it, simply obeying Drax's instruction to pour Sadie a cup of coffee while Drax went to get dressed.

As soon as she had emptied the small cup Ahmed lifted the coffee pot to refill it, but Sadie shook her head and hastily covered her empty cup with her hand, to indicate to him that she didn't want any more. If she kept on drinking such a strong brew she would be on a caffeine-induced high for the rest of the day. But at least thinking about how dreadful it must have been for Drax and his brother to cope with the deaths of their parents gave her something to help her stop focusing on the memory of his nakedness.

She was not the kind of woman who wasted her time mentally dwelling on naked male flesh. Or was she? Wouldn't it be more honest to admit that she hadn't *previously* been that kind of woman?

She was aware, so much aware, that those tiny tingling shudders of 'being aware' were still pulsing dangerously inside her—like a kettle simmering just off the boil, just waiting for that touch to turn up the heat, and then… She could feel the beading of sweat breaking out at her hairline.

This was crazy. She couldn't be obsessing sexually about a man she had only just met. A man who spoke so glowingly to her about his brother that she could be forgiven for thinking that he was actually trying encourage her to fall for *him,* if such a scenario wasn't totally unlikely. A man more unlikely to become her lover it was possible to imagine.

Her lover? She *was* crazy. She had to be. Who had said anything about her wanting a lover? She didn't do lovers. She never had. And she certainly didn't go around fantasising about arrogant ruling princes taking her to bed and making love to her. But just thinking about Drax's tanned, naked body spread against the whiteness of her sheets set her mind racing. What would it feel like to straddle him and keep him there on her bed while she slowly explored the muscular contours of his shoulders and torso? Would he allow her to dominate him like that and take her visual pleasure of him without seeking to master her? Would he let her slowly stroke her way along the byways of his body?

She made a small choking sound of rejection and disbelief in her throat as she tried to disown her thoughts.

'You would perhaps like water?' Ahmed offered her solicitously.

'What? No. Oh, yes, please,' Sadie answered with a quick smile. Perhaps a glass of water might cool her overheated thoughts as it soothed her throat.

Walking through his bedroom, which was as elegantly minimalist as the rest of his quarters, Drax paused in his dressing room to remove clean clothes and then walked into his bathroom, shrugging off his towelling robe as he did so.

He showered quickly, almost brusquely, refusing to focus on his body in any way as he put up a mental barrier to stop himself from thinking about Sadie and the effect she had had on him earlier. But, while he could control his thoughts, he couldn't hide from himself the knowledge that both the ache and its urgency were still there, and that were she to come to him now...

Were she to *what?* Angrily he reached for a towel, jerking it off the heated towel rail. What the hell was he letting himself think that for? She was nothing to him—less than nothing. She was just someone he could use to solve his brother's current problem.

So he wasn't going to mind when Vere took her to bed? Vere probably *wouldn't be* taking her to bed; all his brother needed to do was persuade her to marry him. He didn't have to consummate the marriage. In fact it would be better if he didn't.

Better for whom? For him? Because he couldn't control the white-hot surge of male blood-lust that possessed him at the thought of his twin touching Sadie? Why should he think something like that? He dropped the towel and strode into his dressing room, pulling on clean clothes—not the white tee shirt and the stone-coloured chinos he had originally intended to wear, but traditional Arab dress instead. Because wearing it would reinforce the barrier he needed to create between him and Sadie?

CHAPTER SEVEN

'AND this, as you may remember from the plans I showed you earlier, is the main building of the complex.'

Sadie nodded her head, glad that she was wearing her sunglasses and had covered her head against the strong sun as she stood next to Drax, looking towards the gleaming, mirror-fronted building that rose up in front of her from the desert floor and was so many storeys high it seemed as though it was trying to reach the sky.

Apart from being able to recognise the central completed building, Sadie couldn't pick out any of the other distinguishing features she had seen on the plans in the vast construction site all around them.

Drax had driven them both here himself, not for the first time surprising Sadie with his preference for informality—or at least what passed for informality for him. Sadie hadn't missed the way people turned to look at him, obviously well aware of who he was.

'This new four-lane highway you see under construction runs from the complex to the airport, with this spur, which they are currently working on, going into Dhurahn city. Dhurahn Financial, as we intend to call the new development, will in effect be a city within a city. It will operate under English mercantile law and have its own judiciary system and buildings. Those who work here will have the option of living within its environs in apartment blocks or of moving out to the coast. We find that many overseas nationals prefer to live by the sea if they can, and so we plan to construct another four-lane highway to a sleeper township on the coast.

'The official language within Dhurahn Financial will be English, but naturally translation services will be provided in much the same way as they are in Brussels. Although *our* system will be rather more state-of-the-art.

'The new city is being constructed on a circle plan. The central building will be ringed with roads and additional rings of buildings, which will be divided into segments of quarters, eighths, then sixteenths and so on as the circles widen. Each segment will have its own national flavour with regard to facilities and food outlets, as we intend to become a global financial meeting point.'

Sadie listened in awe. The sheer scale of the plan was breathtaking now that she was here at its centre.

'No one will ever have seen anything like it,' she said.

'No,' Drax agreed calmly. 'That is our plan: that it shall be unique and remain unique. In order to maintain security we intend to operate a chip and pin pass system for everyone who works here. No one will be allowed to enter Dhurahn Financial without the correct authority. Now, let me show you inside the main building.'

As they walked towards it Sadie could see a fleet of immaculate mini-coaches parked outside the main entrance.

'We have been inviting certain financial sector personnel to come to Dhurahn for inspection tours,' Drax explained.

'You've done so much already. I can't see why you would need to employ someone like me,' Sadie told him impetuously, turning to him as she spoke, and then giving a small gasp as her foot slipped on the rubble underfoot.

Drax reacted immediately, reaching out to take hold of her bare arm to steady her.

She was so close to him that she was convinced he must be able to hear the frantic thudding of her heart, never mind see the swift rise and fall of her breasts as she gulped in air. She was suddenly aware that her fingers were clutching at his forearm. The white cotton of his robe felt crisp and fresh beneath the hot stickiness of her hand. She could smell the elusive but sensual scent of male skin and sunshine, and some subtly pleasant cologne; it enticed her to move closer to him so that she could breathe it in. She had taken a step towards him before she could stop herself.

The hand he had placed on her arm moved up to her shoulder, to accommodate her move forward. She could feel its warmth cupping the rounded ball of her shoulder joint where her bare skin met the cotton edge of her top's short sleeve—only his hand wasn't on her sleeve, it was on her bare flesh, as though he had slid his fingers beneath the edge of her sleeve. Just thinking of that kind of intimacy made her tremble as though a fine thread inside her linking every erogenous zone she possessed had been pulled tighter. She could see the dark column of his throat, its skin taut and golden. If she lifted her gaze a little higher she would be able to see his mouth.

Her heart missed one beat and then another as she did exactly that. She couldn't remember ever studying a man's mouth so closely before, or wanting to do so. If she had, the moment was completely overwhelmed now by the experience of absorbing every tiny detail of Drax's mouth. His bottom lip was full and curved, indenting sharply into the corners. She wanted to touch it, to draw her fingertip slowly along it. She wanted... She wanted to lean forward and press her own mouth against his. She wanted...

Did she know what she was doing, looking at him like that? Looking at his mouth with those big eyes, their gaze drowned in open desire? Drax's fingers tightened on the warm, bare flesh of her shoulder, where he had slipped his hand beneath her sleeve, kneading and caressing its curve. He looked down at her body and saw how her nipples were pressing against the fabric of her top, signalling her arousal. It would be the easiest thing in the world to lift his free hand to shape them and then pluck erotically at the boldly aroused flesh, to whisper to her how he would kiss and caress its nakedness before taking it into his mouth to unite them in fierce physical pleasure.

The easiest thing, and the most dangerous. The erection he had controlled earlier throbbed urgently with aching need. He could take her back to his car now. They would be back within the palace and the privacy of his own quarters within half an hour, and then he could take his pleasure of her in all the ways his body was demanding.

Except that he had vowed that she would be Vere's. *Vere's*—not his!

He released her so swiftly that Sadie wasn't sure if what she was feeling was relief or disappointment. What had possessed her to simply stand there like that? she wondered uncomfortably as she tried to keep pace with Drax's long stride. Was it possible that somewhere deep inside every sensible woman there was a throwback gene to a more primitive age, with a secret desire to be claimed by a man strong enough, daring enough and powerful enough, to snatch her up and make her his own?

'It is a pity that my brother isn't here to show you round the building. I am sure that when he returns he will wish to do so. This venture is very close to his heart.'

'But the design concept for the overall plan is yours?' Sadie guessed intuitively, as they reached the entrance to the building.

She didn't want Drax to bring his brother into the conversation. Somehow it broke the intimacy between them, almost as though he was actually physically standing between them. The sharp stab of jealousy she felt shocked her. What kind of foolishness was this? Surely only a woman teetering on the verge of falling wildly and passionately in love with a man could feel jealous of a brother she had yet to meet?

Drax was holding the door to the building open for her. Relieved to have an excuse not to pursue her unwanted line of thought, Sadie stepped through it, shivering a little at the chill of the air-conditioning.

As she gazed upwards from the spacious ground floor with its inner atrium, Sadie couldn't help but be impressed. She knew from the plans Drax had shown her earlier that the building had its own state-of-the-art health club complex, complete with a gym, a swimming pool, treatment rooms, and a restaurant. It also had a cinema that could be used for conferences as well as to show the latest films, several bars and restaurants, and off-duty meeting rooms for the use of those who worked in it. And this was only one of the planned buildings that would form the whole complex.

'What do you think?'

Sadie was astonished that Drax felt he needed to ask her opinion.

'With a set-up like this you're bound to be able to attract top-quality personnel,' she told him honestly. 'I can't imagine anyone turning down the opportunity to work here and be part of such an exciting new venture.'

'We've tried to plan for all contingencies. Some of the more senior personnel will be older, with families, so we're planning to open schools in the new complex on the coast. Dhurahn already has a university, originally endowed and established by our grandfather, but my brother has taken on its expansion as a personal project. He is the philanthropist, while I am more the hard-headed business-man. I think when you meet him that you will find Vere is very much more on your wave-length than I.'

Sadie tensed. For some reason she was beginning to feel almost hostile at Drax's frequent references to his brother's virtues—although she knew there was no logical reason why she should feel that way.

As they waited for a lift to take them to the upper floors Drax's mobile rang. He turned aside to answer it at the same time as the lift doors opened to disgorge a group of European men in business suits, all of them young and, to Sadie, very obviously what she privately termed 'trading floor types'. They exuded the male confidence, arrogance and street cred that epitomised the City boy, and Sadie wasn't surprised to find herself being openly inspected.

That didn't bother her particularly, but she felt far less sanguine when one of them suddenly detached himself from the others and came over to her, saying loudly in an over-familiar way that infuriated her, 'Well, if it isn't Sadie! Prim little Sadie, who doesn't do sex. What brings you here? You can't be up for a job. They only want the top graduates—although Lord knows you must need the money since you got the push from the bank.'

To Sadie's relief Drax, still speaking into his mobile, was standing too far away to hear what was being said, although he had turned round to face them.

'Actually, I already have a job, thank you, Jack,' Sadie answered as calmly as she could.

Jack Logan. Jack the Lad, as the other men in the office had admiringly nick-named him. Sadie had disliked him from the moment they had been introduced—and she had ended up disliking him even more after he had trapped her in an empty office and tried to coerce her into having sex with him. Luckily she had managed to escape before he had tried to force her, but Sadie knew that he hadn't forgiven her for rejecting him. His comments now were, she acknowledged, a form of payback.

Drax had finished his conversation and was looking enquiringly at her. Sadie wriggled past her unpleasant former colleague and hurried over to rejoin him.

'An old friend?' Drax asked her coolly.

'We used to work together,' Sadie answered shortly, wondering what Jack the Lad would make of the deference being shown to Drax by his guide as he salaamed with deep reverence and Drax responded with a small inclination of his head.

'And this, of course, is the main dealing room.'

Sadie nodded her head in acknowledgement as they completed their tour of the building. As yet the vast room did not reek of male hormones and the sharp scent of bullish aggression, like the dealing rooms she was used to, but no doubt they soon would.

'That young man you were talking to earlier,' Drax demanded abruptly. 'What exactly is your relationship?'

If the question had come from anyone else, Sadie knew she would have refused to answer it. But she was becoming used to Drax's autocratic belief that he had a right to have even his most intimate questions answered. Either that or her emotions were becoming so entrapped by him that she wanted him to know everything about her and her past. Though of course she wasn't silly enough to let herself get emotionally involved with a man who had shown no signs of wanting an involvement, was she?

'As I've already told you, we worked together.'

'His body language suggested that his relationship with you was more than that of a mere work colleague,' Drax said.

Sadie shook her head. 'The young men from the trading floor always behave like that. It's part of their macho image; it doesn't mean anything.'

'So you weren't involved in a sexual relationship with him?' Drax persisted.

He wasn't asking these questions on his own account, he assured himself. Why should he be? After all it was of no interest to him how many men had taken her to bed. No, he was thinking of his brother.

He knew Vere would never accept as his wife a woman whose ex-lover was the kind of man he had seen talking to Sadie—even as his temporary wife. It was unrealistic, of course, to expect her not to have had a sexual partner—even more than one—but the people of Dhurahn would have certain expectations about the wives of their rulers, and those expectations would have to be met—even if its rulers knew the marriage was only going to be temporary.

'No, I wasn't,' Sadie reaffirmed, almost fiercely. Was her face burning as much as she thought? Betraying how uncomfortable she felt? It wasn't that she had anything to hide, or at least not the kind of thing that her employer seemed to think she might have to hide, but she was acutely sensitive about the fact that for a woman of her age and situation she was lacking the kind of sexual experience she might be expected to have. There probably never had been an age when a woman in her twenties was proud to say openly that she was still a virgin; in earlier times, when female virginity had been prized, girls had been married in their teens, and unmarried virgins past that age would probably have been looked upon as objects of pity—rejects, unable to find a husband and bringing shame on her family.

Now, while it was laughable that any woman should feel rejected because she wasn't married, there was a certain stigma—a certain sniggering kind of unkindness, especially from men—attached to a woman who remained a virgin.

Sadie could well imagine how someone like Jack Logan would react if he knew the truth about her. Which was, of course, why she had made sure that no one did know, keeping her secret to herself.

It wasn't as if she had made some kind of

vow to cling to celibacy—far from it. It was just that the right partner had never come along at the right time, and then, when she had begun to realise that she might have left it later than normal to lose her virginity, she had started to worry about how any potential partner might react to the knowledge that he was to be her first lover. That in turn had caused her to keep the men she did date at arm's length, so that the whole situation had grown steadily more burdensome—rather like compound interest, she told herself with grim humour.

Drax watched her, wondering what it was causing the defensive and almost secretive look to darken her eyes, and what it was she was so obviously withholding from him. There could, of course, be only one thing. She was lying to him about her relationship with the man he had seen talking to her. Normally the knowledge that a woman was lying to him about her sexual past would have caused him to feel merely cynically amused. But, as he was slowly being forced to recognise, nothing that had happened to him since he had first set eyes on Sadie came anywhere near being close to his 'normal' reaction. That alone was enough to infuriate him, without the added thought of Sadie with another man. He could see her now, giving herself to that man with wanton abandon, inciting him with her soft full mouth and her sweetly curved body to take them to the savage erotic heights he himself so ached to show her.

Drax fought desperately to ignore what he was feeling and thinking. But it was too late. As surely as any genie let loose from its imprisoning bottle, the reality of his desire for her had been exposed.

'We need to return to the palace,' he told her curtly. 'I have a meeting I need to attend.'

There wasn't any meeting, but he didn't trust himself to remain alone with her in his present mood, and at least if they returned to the palace he could distance himself from her.

Sadie was too relieved that he had stopped questioning her about her non-existent sex-life to worry about his brusque manner.

They were waiting for the lift when the man who had been escorting Jack Logan's group came hurrying towards them, salaaming to Drax and then saying something urgently to him in Arabic.

'Go downstairs and wait for me in the

foyer,' Drax told Sadie after he had listened to the older man. 'There is something I have to attend to. I won't be very long.'

Nodding her head, Sadie got in the lift.

The foyer really was magnificent, she acknowledged, as she stepped out of the lift on the ground floor. Drax and his brother were bound to make a success of their venture, and she admitted that she hoped there might be a real future for her here.

Although Dhurahn, like Zuran, was a modern city, there was still that awareness of the proximity of the desert and its mystery, and she had learned while she was in Zuran that there was something about it that enthralled her. She had taken a couple of organised trips out to the *wadis,* and had marvelled at everything she had seen, gaining respect for the strength and pride of those who had lived for so many centuries in this hostile but strangely beautiful environment. If she were allowed to stay on she would try to explore the desert a little more, get to know more about it, she told herself, letting her thoughts drift as she waited patiently for Drax.

When she at last heard the hum of the descending lift she waited expectantly for the doors to open—only to stiffen with shock when it wasn't Drax who got out, but Jack Logan. He was grinning wolfishly at her in the almost obscenely vain way he had that she had always found so threatening.

'I saw you get in the lift, so I thought I'd come down and keep you company,' he said mockingly. 'How did you manage to get involved with the top man, by the way? Not via his bed, I'll bet... You wouldn't have lasted two seconds there once he'd sussed out how sexless you are...'

Sadie swung round, turning her back on him, praying that Drax would appear and unwittingly rescue her from her tormentor.

'Sadie, Sadie...' Jack Logan was singing softly. 'Who won't open her legs for anyone. What's it like being so uptight? Tell you what I'll do, seeing as I'm feeling generous, I'll show you what it's like to have a man...'

If she just ignored him he'd get tired of harassing her and leave her alone, Sadie reasoned. If she just stood here and avoided eye contact— She gave a shocked protest when Jack suddenly grabbed hold of her and swung her round. He was considered good-looking, she knew, but he had mean eyes, and the cruel look in them made her shudder.

'You thought you were so clever, making a fool of me in London—didn't you? Well, now it's your turn. Now it's payback time, Sadie.'

This couldn't be happening to her. Not in broad daylight, here in this beautiful building. But it was. Jack Logan was laughing at her as he held on to her, and then he reached out and squeezed her breast. When she shuddered with loathing and closed her eyes he laughed even more.

Sadie didn't hear the lift door opening. Nor did she see the look on Drax's face when he saw her standing with her back to him in another man's embrace, another man touching her. But Jack saw Drax, and he saw the look in his eyes, so he bent his head and kissed Sadie fiercely and unkindly on her tightly closed lips, before releasing her and saying softly, 'Like I said, it's payback time,' then sauntering off, leaving her to take a deep breath and wipe her hand across her mouth in an attempt to wipe the taste and the feel of him from her memory.

'If you're ready?'

The icy coldness in Drax's voice made her turn towards him, her eyes still dark with shocked distress.

She felt too numb to say anything, much less attempt to explain what had happened as she fell into step beside him, struggling to match his long, impatient stride as he hurried her back to his car.

It wasn't on his own account that he was filled with such ferocious and all-consuming anger, Drax assured himself. No, it was because her behaviour, as he had just witnessed it, had proved her to be a liar and a sexual adventuress—and thus totally unfit to become Vere's wife. That meant bringing her here to Dhurahn had been a complete waste of his time, and time wasn't something Drax liked to waste.

He strode ahead of Sadie without bothering to turn and check that she was able to negotiate the rubble safely. Not because his anger had wiped out his good manners, but because he simply did not trust himself to speak to her, never mind touch her right now. How could she have allowed that oaf to maul her like that? And in public. Where he could see them. In *his* country, where such displays of sexual intimacy were an offence in the eyes of some of his more devout people. She had behaved with a complete lack of respect—for his country, for him, and for herself. Normally that would have been enough to thoroughly disgust him. Normally?

He *was* disgusted, Drax assured himself as he yanked open the driver's door to his car. Disgusted and bitterly, dangerously angry. So angry, in fact, that... That what? he challenged himself as Sadie slid into the passenger seat of the car. He could smell the scent of her skin, and with it her fear. Her *fear?* Surely she should have smelled of her boyfriend and the intimacy they had been sharing?

Drax didn't trust himself to look at her. Because he was jealous of the fact that she had given herself to another man?

No!

Sadie sat rigidly in her seat, trying to focus on the view ahead and stop herself from giving in to her emotions. Inwardly she felt nauseous and shivery, shaking with loathing and horror from Jack's touch. And sickeningly aware of just how much he had enjoyed humiliating her in the way that he had.

Thank goodness Drax had come along when he did—because if he hadn't... She tried to tell herself that she was over-dramatising what had happened, and that Jack had simply been tormenting her. He surely wouldn't have gone as far as actually...raping her? She shuddered violently, gritting her teeth against the whimper of horror bubbling inside her.

Drax saw her small shiver and automatically turned down the air-conditioning. He could see the goosebumps on her arms. She was staring into the distance, no doubt wishing she was still with her lover, imagining what they could be doing. He cursed savagely under his breath. He couldn't believe the extent of his own misjudgement. He, who had always prided himself on his swift and accurate assessment of a person's true character. She hadn't even had the grace to attempt to make an excuse for herself, never mind apologise for the lies she had told him.

They had reached the palace, and the guards salaamed them in through the heavy gates. What was she thinking now? Did she imagine he was simply going to ignore her conduct— and her lies? If so, she was speedily going to discover her error.

He brought the car to a halt and switched off the engine, saying curtly, 'Come with me. There is something I wish to discuss with you.'

Numbly, Sadie nodded her head. She had no

idea what Drax wanted to say to her, but she hoped that whatever it was it would be compelling enough to help her stop reliving what had happened with Jack Logan. Her breast actually felt slightly sore where he had squeezed it. Sore and dirty... Everything felt dirty... Every bit of her, inside and out, and not just her body, but her thoughts as well—as though somehow he had contaminated all of her with his disgusting behaviour.

CHAPTER EIGHT

IT FELT as though days rather than hours had passed since she had last stood in this room, Sadie reflected as she stood in the middle of Drax's private sitting room, looking out towards the swimming pool.

Drax had brought her here and then told her to wait, disappearing in the direction of what she assumed must be his bedroom.

This time he hadn't asked her if she wanted anything to eat or drink, and the truth was that she felt desperately in need of a reviving caffeine boost. Instead she had to make do with what water was left in the bottle she had taken out with her earlier. Now lukewarm, it tasted slightly brackish.

Drax would have to tell Sadie that she was dismissed. He had no other option now, knowing that she had made contact with what was obviously a past lover here in Dhurahn. There was no way that Vere could be allowed to marry her. It was unthinkable. His only option was to pay her off and put her on the first flight back to London, her lover with her.

The supposedly calming, cool shower he'd just had had done nothing to lessen the boiling heat of his emotions. He reached for a towel to dry himself and then changed his mind, instead pulling on the fresh towelling robe that his manservant had left ready for him. He headed barefoot into the room where he had left Sadie.

Sadie was standing facing the window, her now empty water bottle clasped tightly in her hands. Drax didn't want his body to react the way it did when he looked at her, but he seemed powerless to stop it. He made a small harsh sound of self-disgust beneath his breath that caused Sadie to turn and look at him, her eyes darkening and her face heating with colour for all the world as though she were re-membering seeing him naked and was embar-rassed that he might know. Drax could taste the bitterness of his own raw emotions.

'You really had me fooled, you know,' he told her with forced calm as he walked towards her. 'When you put on that act for me, pretending to be shocked by Monika's suggestion that you seduce her clients, I fell for it completely. When you told me that the grinning ape you were encouraging was merely a business acquaintance, I believed you.'

'I told you the truth,' Sadie said. This was not what she had expected to hear him say, and she couldn't conceal her shock.

'Liar! I saw the way you were letting him touch you.'

Her emotional radar registered his banked-down fury, but she couldn't understand what had caused it.

'I saw the intimacy between you,' he continued harshly, adding savagely as he caught hold of her, '*This* kind of intimacy.'

He was holding her as he had done earlier, his hands sliding beneath the capped sleeves of her top to grip the rounded curve of her shoulders. But this time he wasn't just holding her, he was kissing her as well—possessing her mouth, forcing her lips to part for the demanding thrust of his tongue. She knew she ought to stop him, to push him away and insist that he listen to her, to demand an apology and a retraction of his accusation, but the need inside her was powering through her, obliterating reason and conscience, ruthlessly silencing every warning voice that would have spoken against it, filling her until there was nothing else—nothing else but his kiss and no one else but him.

What was happening to him? Somehow Sadie had taken the kiss he had begun as a savage indictment of her duplicity, allowing a safe escape for his own anger, and turned it into something different—something so sensually sweet and magical that his desire for her was drawing him under like a swimmer caught in a powerful undertow. He could neither resist it nor escape it. It called out to him with a siren song that lured him into waters so treacherous that he was already lost.

When he let go of her she reached for him and drew him closer, encircling him with her arms around his neck, tangling her tongue with his in a slow dance of rebirth from which they would emerge not as two separate people but as one. He slid his hand beneath her shirt, spanning her back and then letting his fingertips trace the narrow sharpness of her collarbone. She felt so fragile, as though he could crush her in his hands, and yet she was so strong—strong enough to overpower him with her sensuality. Her tongue-tip touched his mouth quickly and delicately, retreating as though shocked by its own boldness, and then returned to taste him again, almost compulsively. His hands slid to her breasts. Inside his head he could see himself touching them whilst she arched back in his hold, her throat tightly corded with desire, the heels of her palms pushing on his shoulders. Another minute and he would be pushing her top out of the way to taste her willing flesh...

Sadie quivered with emotion as Drax's hands tightened on her breasts. It felt so good to have him holding her like this, to feel his touch burning away the loathsome memory of Jack Logan. She wanted to beg him to take away all the barriers between them, to hold her so that from now on when she closed her eyes and thought of today all she would be able to remember was him. She didn't know how they had got to this level of intimacy so swiftly, and she didn't want to know. All she wanted was to be burned clean and purified by the fierce heat of their mutual passion. Her ability to think logically was wholly suspended, overridden by the demands of a new command centre. All she wanted was for Drax to take her to bed... No, all she wanted was for Drax to simply take her, she amended dizzily. To take her completely and totally—here, now, at once. Eagerly she pressed herself into his hands and his body, lifting her own hands to hold his head while she kissed him over and over again, whispering to him how much she wanted him.

This was madness, Drax knew. But why should he not have her? She was offering herself to him, he wanted her, and with what he knew about her now she could never marry Vere. Why shouldn't he have her? Why *shouldn't* he take her as she was begging him to do?

There were a thousand reasons why he shouldn't—but they weren't enough to outweigh the one compelling, compulsive reason why he must. So he lifted his hands from her breasts, swung her up into his arms and carried her into his bedroom. Sadie wrapped her arms around his neck and kissed his jawline and his throat, then pushed aside the neck of his robe to kiss his collarbone, so that by the time he had reached the bed she was so high on his scent and taste that no power on earth could have matched the intensity of her desire for him.

Drax lowered her onto the bed, pausing only to shrug off his robe, and Sadie gazed up at him, marvelling at his male beauty as he arched over her. With her fingertip she traced the corded sinews of his arms, wondering at their male strength beneath the satin heat of his skin. His chest was dark with fine hair which arrowed downwards, causing her heart to leap high inside her chest and then beat unsteadily and too fast as she remembered the way she had felt that morning when she had watched him emerging from the pool. The water had run from his chest straight down that dark line, and she had followed its journey and seen, as she could see now, the base of the stiffening evidence of his desire for her. Sadie trembled as she leaned forward and kissed the base of his throat.

Drax arched against the caress of her mouth, not knowing why that kiss and this woman should affect him so immediately and so fiercely that he could feel his reaction right down to his toes.

As she kissed him he undressed her, feeling

her slip eagerly and easily from her clothes and into his hands. Even now her mouth was still pressed against his skin. She had fantasised about this, Sadie acknowledged dizzily, and now somehow Drax was lying on his back and she was above him, instinctively straddling him. The reality was a hundred—no, a thousand times more erotic than her imaginings, and if she closed her eyes how much more intense would the sensation of Drax's hands on her body be? But she couldn't bear not to see him, not to watch him as he touched her and she touched him. And she wanted so much to touch him…so desperately *had* to touch him.

She leaned forward until her hair swung down to shield her face and stroke Drax's body. But he could still see her expression. She touched him in a way that no woman had ever touched him before, eagerly and yet unknowingly, as though everything about what she was doing was new to her, as though she was following her instincts rather than her experience. When her fingers touched him and then curled around him he felt her hesitate. She looked at him as though seeking reassurance, and then, when he gave it, he could see her confidence grow—and with it her need. It was as though she hungered desperately for him—as though the touching filled her with intense delight and yet fed her need for more of him.

In her eyes was a look of wondering and amazed delight. It curved her mouth and somehow filled the air between them, so that he could almost taste it himself. Nothing he had done before had been like this. Or like her… Whatever magic spell she had cast it had pulled him under its influence, he admitted, as he caught hold of her free hand and lifted it to his mouth, kissing each finger in turn and then licking her soft palm. He watched as her nipples tightened and her belly quivered, and beneath her closed eyelids welled tears of intense arousal.

He reached for her, his hands on her waist, lifting her and steadying her, his fingers digging into her flesh when he felt her hesitation.

She moistened her lips with the tip of her tongue, her voice husky and uncertain as she said, 'I'm not… I don't… Oughtn't we to…?'

He was tight and hot and hard with a surging need that didn't want to wait.

'Oughtn't we to what?' he demanded.

'You know…use something. For…for safe sex and…' She was blushing now. She could feel the heat burning her skin. 'And to make sure that I don't… I mean… I'm sorry,' she told him simply, 'but I haven't done this before.'

How could he feel such anger and yet still want her? He pushed her away and sat up in the large bed,

'What on earth are you saying? We both know that is a lie,' he said savagely. 'No woman your age hasn't "done this before",' he told her scornfully, mimicking the soft uncertainty of her voice. 'I wouldn't believe it even if I *hadn't* seen you letting your lover maul you with my own eyes.'

'Letting him… I wasn't letting him do anything!' Sadie said, filled with shocked disbelief that he should speak to her that way after the intimacy they had been sharing. 'For your information—not that you're going to believe me, and it's obvious that you don't *want* to believe me—'

Her voice had started to tremble poignantly, and she had to fight to control it. 'He grabbed hold of me and wouldn't let me go. And he *isn't* my lover. He never has been. *That's* why he did it. For revenge. He told me that.'

Even now, having heard the antagonism and rejection in Drax's voice, seen it in his eyes, she still couldn't fully take on board what was happening. She had heard the emotion and felt the tears threatening to break through into her voice as she'd tried to deal with Drax's verbal attack. How could things have changed so quickly? Was this what men did when they took you to bed and then changed their minds about wanting you? Did they seize on some imagined shortcoming instead of being honest? He had left behind their shared intimacy, abandoning it as speedily as he had abandoned her; she was still struggling to release herself from it. Her mind and her emotions might be trying to deal with the hurt Drax had caused her, but her body was still aching for satisfaction. Her pain was still mercifully at the brutally numbing stage, when she knew that it was going to hurt but the shock of it was still too great for her to feel it.

Sadie couldn't be what she was claiming to be. It just wasn't possible. But there was something about the look in her eyes that shamed him. And his body was reminding him of how innocent and untutored her touch had been.

Innocent? he taunted himself. After the intimacy she had shown him? Intimacy, yes, but an intimacy full of desire and longing—the kind of intimacy that was devoid of skilled experience but which reached right to the heart of the man being shown it. And wasn't that why he was feeling the way he was? Torn apart by a toxic mix of anger, rejection of what his heart was telling him, and the fear of having gone too far in a direction he couldn't afford to take?

Why didn't Drax say something? Anything to show that he was listening to her, really listening to her and absorbing what she was saying.

In desperation Sadie said fiercely, 'Jack Logan is the kind of man who thinks that every women he meets ought to find him attractive. When I made it plain to him that I didn't he started to see me as some kind of challenge.'

She had tugged free some of the bedding and was now holding it protectively in front of her, to hide herself from him. The shame inside him drove deeper. For some reason her need to cover herself touched something sharply painful inside him. He wanted to go to her, and hold her, take the look of bleak pain and hurt pride from her eyes. He wanted to take *her* back in his arms and tell her how precious and rare what they shared was.

He wanted to finish what they had started. But how could he now? Her reminder about the need for them to practise safe sex had brought him back to reality. If she wasn't lying, if she was as untouched as she was claiming, then that meant...

That meant she was Vere's.

The choice was his. He could take her back to bed, find out for himself if she was speaking the truth and then face the consequences. Or he could question her companion before he left the country. There was a sour, bitter taste in his mouth. His pride jerked against the thought of humbling himself enough to do such a thing. But he had to do it. He had to know. Not for his own sake, and not even for hers, but for Vere's. The loyalty he owed his brother came before anything and anyone else.

'Get dressed and go back to your quarters,' he told Sadie curtly. 'We'll discuss this further later.'

CHAPTER NINE

WAS she really so weak that she was actually allowing Drax to treat her like this? Sadie derided herself angrily an hour later, as she sat alone in what should have been the tranquillity of the private gardens of the women's quarters. Why hadn't she objected when he had virtually ordered her to come here? Why hadn't she refused and told him that she wanted to leave Dhurahn immediately? What was wrong with her?

Did she really need to ask herself that? What was wrong with her was the same thing that afflicted every woman who had ever fallen in love with the wrong man for the wrong reasons.

Fallen in love? Where had those words come from? She hadn't fallen in love with Drax! No? Then what was the motivation behind her current driving compulsive need to be with him, to hold him and touch him, to talk with him and learn all about him, to open her heart and mind to him, to take his hand and cling to it while they walked together though the shadows of her past, to give him the intimacy of herself and to be given the same intimacy back from him? What was all that if not love? How could she deny to herself that this was how she felt? But how could she love him when she knew that he did not feel the same way? And how was she going to deal with that and protect herself from its pain?

It had been a simple enough matter for Drax to delay the return flight to Heathrow carrying the young bankers and MBAs who had leapt so eagerly at the chance to come to Dhurahn. He was actually in the terminal building when the Royal flight bringing his twin home a day ahead of schedule touched down—although he was not aware of Vere's arrival.

Jack Logan wasn't at all concerned at the delay in their flight's departure—the only thing that hadn't run to schedule in the whole of their superbly organised and tightly packed trip. He was quite happy to while away the time demanding more of the vintage champagne being served by the pretty hostesses, at the same time subjecting them to some heavily explicit flirtation. Nor was he too concerned when an immaculately dressed middle-aged official came to escort him off the plane. To the cat-calls, whoops and cheers of his companions, the older man explained to him that there was a small irregularity that needed to be dealt with.

'Small, is it, Jack?' one of his friends called out coarsely. 'And there's you always boasting that it's six inches and rising.'

'Nah—six inches *without* rising,' Jack quipped back over his shoulder, grinning at the pretty hostess standing by the exit.

By the time he was actually shown into Drax's presence ten minutes later he was swaggering boastfully, and blustering out an arrogant demand to be told what the hell was going on.

'Forgive me for the inconvenience,' Drax apologised calmly. 'I assure you that you will soon be free to rejoin your flight. You know Ms Sadie Murray?'

Since Drax was now in western dress, and speaking very calmly, Jack had no sense of being in any danger. Nor did he make the association between the traditionally dressed man he had seen with Sadie and the urbane authority of this man seated in front of him. He immediately leapt to the conclusion that Sadie had lodged a complaint against him. The better part of a bottle of champagne had dulled his normally sharp awareness of how to protect his interests, and led him now to laugh and say unkindly, 'Yes, I know her. She's the type that acts like she's wearing a chastity belt and enjoying it. As sexless as it's possible for a woman to be.'

'You saw her earlier on today, I believe?' Drax continued, outwardly ignoring Jack's swaggering manner but inwardly registering every betraying word and look.

'Yeah, I saw her. Ms Don't-touch-me,' he told Drax mockingly, and then swore crudely before continuing, 'God, but I really hate her smugness. If anyone has it coming to her, she does. Acting like she's too good for me.'

There was an ugly look in his eyes, and Drax had to swallow hard against the sour taste in his mouth as he realised the danger Sadie had been in. 'You wanted to show her who was boss? Scare her a bit...punish her?' he suggested.

'Yeah, right.' Jack was warming more and more to his interrogator by the second. 'She deserved it. Turning me down like she did. I'd have been a fool not to take the opportunity to pay her back.'

'So you slipped away from the others and followed her?'

'Yeah. She's complained about me, has she? That's typical of her. Just because I gave her a bit of a scare. If I'd been that desperate I'd have found myself a woman who knows what it's all about—not some prim, innocent virgin-type like her.' He gave a contemptuous shrug. 'Man, what a turn-off she is. But she owed me, and she had it coming to her.'

How could he not have believed Sadie? Drax was torn between a need to walk—no, *run* from the small enclosed room and go straight to her, and a savage urge to grab Jack by the throat and tell him what he thought of him. Instead he had to conceal what he was actually thinking and ask pleasantly, 'What do you mean, she had it coming to her?'

Jack Logan grimaced. 'She turned me down and made me look a fool, so it was payback time. Come on, mate, *you* must know what it's all about when a woman acts that way.'

'What way do you mean?' Drax asked.

'You know. She made out that I was some kind of pervert just because I made a bit of a play for her, and threatened to complain if I did it again. So I thought I'd pay her back for it.'

'Frighten her, you mean?' It was an effort for Drax to keep his voice empty of emotion and to offer Jack a small, man-to-man conspiratorial smile.

Jack was starting to relax. This was a man's man, he could tell—the type who understood what life was all about.

'Yeah, that's right. Okay, so I grabbed hold of her and touched her up a bit. If she's fool enough to make a big deal of it then that's her problem. Anyway, don't you have a law out here about women being guilty as hell if they get themselves raped?'

Drax decided he would very much like to tear Jack Logan limb from limb and throw his body to the desert vultures to pick clean. But of course he could do no such thing.

'Thank you for your time, Mr Logan,' he said distantly. 'You will now be escorted back to your plane.'

Jack stood up and gave him a lewd grin.

'Great—I've got one of those pretty little

trolley dollies all set up, ready and waiting to go.'

Drax made a mental note to make sure that the cabin crew were warned to keep a close watch on him on the return flight—but his thoughts were really on Sadie and how fast he could get back to her and apologise.

Sadie hadn't realised that there was another entrance into the garden until she saw Drax walking towards her from the opposite end to her own quarters. He was wearing traditional robes, the sunlight falling across his arrogantly handsome face.

Her heart leapt and then abruptly stopped leaping, and then did nothing except beat in its normal way. Even when Drax was standing within a few feet of her, looking at her with that small, half curling twist of his lips that normally sent her heart-rate into overdrive and turned her weak with longing, she didn't want him. She felt like pinching herself, just to make sure she could feel something and hadn't somehow gone completely numb. How could she not feel *anything?* But she didn't. Not a single throb of desire or an ache of longing, not a single inclination to run to him, not even the anger she had every right to feel after the way he had treated her. Which meant... Which meant that she didn't love him after all. She was safe; she no longer needed to worry. And yet...

'If you've come to apologise—' she said fiercely.

'I do owe you an apology, it is true.' He was inclining his head slightly, his voice cool and remote, almost as though...

'You aren't Drax,' she accused, not knowing really why she should say it or how it could be true, and yet at the same time utterly convinced that she was right.

'No,' he agreed. 'I'm not Drax. I'm his brother—Vere. And you, of course, are Ms Sadie Murray?'

'Yes,' Sadie said, suddenly feeling rather self-conscious.

'I must congratulate you, Ms Murray. Very few people can tell Drax and I apart, even though they may have known us for years. You, on the other hand, perceived almost instantly that I was not my brother.'

'I don't know why I said that,' Sadie admitted. 'You look like him.'

'Actually, *he* looks like *me,* since I am older.

But, yes, we are identical.' He smiled at her. 'You will forgive me, I hope, if—having introduced myself to you and bade you welcome to our country and our home—I make my excuses?'

'Yes. Yes of course.'

The wonder wasn't that she had realised he wasn't Drax, but that she had ever imagined he might be, Sadie reflected as she watched him leave. They might look identical, but in character and manner they were very different. Vere was so much more formal than Drax, so much more reserved and withdrawn. Just as arrogant, no doubt, but stiffer, more wary and 'ruler-like'. And, of course, not anywhere near so desirable as Drax. But she had already warned herself that she must not love him.

How much more easy her life would be if Drax was more like his twin and she didn't want him, Sadie reflected ruefully, as she watched the goldfish swimming lazily amongst the water lilies in the pond.

On his way back to the palace all Drax could think about was Sadie. He had been wrong in refusing to believe her, but right in recognising that the real motivation for his anger hadn't been so much that he had thought she was lying as the fact that he had begun to realise his true feelings for her.

Vere, no doubt, would be highly amused when Drax informed him that he intended to take his advice and marry Sadie himself. But, instead of her being a temporary wife, he wanted her to be his permanent wife—his one and only wife, the wife of his heart.

He drove faster than normal, anxious to get back to Sadie, and the first thing he did when he reached the palace was to make his way straight to the women's quarters.

Sadie had come inside, out of the heat of the sun, to have a cooling shower and drink the glass of mint tea Hakeem had brought for her. When she heard the faint tap on the door to her suite, she thought at first it must be the maid—until the door opened and Drax strode in, closing it firmly behind him.

This time her heart knew exactly who he was. She longed to throw herself into his arms. But she hadn't forgotten the cruel things he had said to her, so she stood tensely, watching him as he came towards her.

'I've come to apologise,' he said simply.

Just the scent of his skin was enough to send

her dizzy with longing and to reactivate the unsatisfied ache he had left deep within her body.

'I've spoken to Jack Logan.' Sadie watched as his mouth tightened and anger flashed darkly in the depths of his eyes. 'He's scum.'

'But you were prepared to believe him when you wouldn't believe me?' Sadie pointed out quietly.

'I was jealous,' Drax said quietly. 'I'm not trying to make excuses for myself, Sadie, but it maddened me to see you in his arms and to think— Jealous men do stupid things; they think stupid things as well. I was wrong, and I should have believed you. Can you forgive me?'

Could she? She already knew the answer to that, and she saw from the way he was looking at her that Drax knew it too.

He was walking very purposefully and determinedly towards her, and there was a gleam in his eyes that warned her of what he was going to do.

'Well?' he whispered huskily as he took her in his arms. 'You haven't answered me yet.'

'I don't know,' Sadie whispered. She couldn't stop looking at him, even though she knew he would read in her eyes how much she loved him. He was going to kiss her...

'Drax—' she began, but she knew she wanted her denial to be too late and ignored.

He was still holding her, and he could feel the unsteady thudding of her heart. 'Are you feeling what I'm feeling?' he asked softly.

'What…what do you mean?'

'You know what I mean. I mean *this*.' He pushed back the sleeve of her robe, stroking his fingertips the length of her inner arm until they rested on the furious race of her pulse.

Sadie could feel her body yearning towards his, wanting him, wanting everything he had denied her earlier.

'And this,' he continued gently, as he raised his hand to brush his fingertips across her throat. 'You love me, don't you?' he demanded.

He was so self-assured, so arrogant, that part of her wanted to be able to deny his words, to shake her head and tell him that he was wrong. But she couldn't. Not when he was teasing tender little kisses along the length of her collarbone, pushing back the neckline of her robe so that it slid off her shoulder, offering up the creamy swell of her naked breasts to his touch, showing him the eager dark flush of her nipples. No wonder he was cupping her breast and teasing her nipple into an even harder peak, tugging it gently with his thumb and forefinger so that it stiffened even more, when her longing arched through her from where he was touching her to the heat of her sex.

'What happens if I say yes?' Sadie asked huskily, made bold by the look in his eyes. A heady euphoria was taking possession of her, encouraging her to dare to tease him in response to that look. It was like learning to dance, Sadie decided a little breathlessly, and suddenly discovering that by some kind of magical empathy your steps were fitting together so well that you moved as one, without hesitation or awkwardness.

'This,' Drax answered her softly, cupping her face in his hands and then stringing tiny kisses along the line of her lips, alternating kisses with the words, 'I love you, Sadie Murray,' so that they became a paean of loving sensuality and desire that dissolved her doubts and melted her resistance.

'In that case, perhaps I should say it,' Sadie whispered back to him. 'I like to hear you telling me that you love me.'

'I think you'd like it even more if I showed you as well as told you,' Drax murmured.

Sadie barely felt the robe being slipped from her shoulders. It was all she could do to respond unsteadily, 'You do?'

'I do,' Drax said, and then he gathered her up in his arms, almost crushing her to him as he kissed her with all the fierce passion she'd been longing for.

The time for teasing and flirting was over.

Could there be anything more heart-soaringly beautiful and meaningful than this? Sadie marvelled as she lay on her bed in Drax's arms while he kissed and caressed her and whispered to her how much he loved her and how sorry he was for ever doubting her.

'I love you so much,' Sadie whispered back. 'I want you so much,' she added truthfully. 'Take off your clothes, Drax, so that I can see you and touch you.'

'You do it,' he urged, taking hold of her hands and placing them on his body. 'While I do this…'

How was she supposed to concentrate on fabrics and fastenings when Drax was kissing his way down the slope of her breast and then sensitising the dark aroused flesh of her nipple to the point of such exquisite and unbearable pleasure that it made her cry out his name?

Wildly Sadie arched up to his mouth, her fingers digging into the hard muscles of his arms as she shuddered in the vortex of the surges of erotic need induced by the sensation of his lips closing round her aroused flesh. She was lost, taken over, filled by the intensity of her own fierce desire. She wanted to hold his head against her breast; she wanted to arch up against him, naked flesh to naked flesh; she wanted to wrap her legs tightly around him and draw him down to her so that he was within her and she was holding him, possessing him, drawing him deeper into that place where she ached for him.

But Drax wasn't responding to her passionate non-verbal pleas. Instead he was smoothing her gently onto the bed and then kissing his way down her body, his hands on her hips, his tongue circling her navel. Shivers of the most exciting and erotic sensation radiated out from where Drax was caressing her. He stroked his fingertips slowly and gently over the tops of her thighs, brushing her skin so lightly and delicately that she immediately yearned for more, for a stronger, more intimate touch. Of their own free will her legs softened and parted, inviting the movement of his hand to cup her sex whilst she closed her eyes to absorb the warm intimacy of his touch.

The pulse of her own need was hot and heavy, so fast and urgent that it was consuming her, making her arch up against his hand, small sounds of longing escaping from her lips until Drax took them from her in a possessive kiss. The tip of his tongue probed gently between her lips, almost mirroring the movement of his fingertip, stroking apart the swollen heaviness of the soft lips that protected her sex. First one and then the other parted in eager welcome, urging him to deeper intimacies. Whilst his tongue meshed and danced with hers, weaving a pattern of erotic enticement, his fingertip stroked the same message of promised delight along the wetness of her sex, until it reached the tight, excited centre of her pleasure.

She cried out, a muffled, almost disbelieving sound, riding the rhythmic storm of her pleasure as it possessed her, leaving her quivering in awed delight in the shelter of his arms.

'I want you, Drax,' she whispered passionately to him. 'I want you inside me. Now...'

His arms tightened around her. She could

feel the hard urgent throb of his erection, and her fingers reached eagerly for it so that she could stroke and caress him. But even though she could feel him growing ready beneath her touch, even though she moved invitingly against him, he did not cover her and take possession of her. Instead, he kissed her tenderly and told her softly, 'Not yet. I love you, Sadie, and I want our first time to be a special pleasure. I want you to marry me, Sadie.'

'Oh, Drax.'

'Is that a yes?' Drax demanded.

When Sadie nodded her head, Drax kissed her tenderly.

'You never told me your brother was your twin,' she accused him as he released her, suddenly remembering that she hadn't yet told him about seeing his brother. 'At first when he walked into the garden I thought he was you. He looks like you. But I knew somehow that he wasn't you—even before he spoke to me.'

'Most people can't tell us apart even when they've known us for a long time.'

'Maybe it's because I love *you* that I can?' Sadie suggested softly. 'Not that it wasn't a bit of a shock to discover that you hadn't warned me that there are two of you.'

'Vere is so much a part of me that I tend to take it for granted, I suppose.'

'You're very close, then?'

Sadie was guiltily aware that a part of her almost wished that Drax wasn't a twin. Why? Was it because knowing he shared such a close relationship with someone else who had been there for him all his life somehow threatened her own relationship with him? How could that happen? She was looking for problems where none existed, she told herself firmly. After all, hadn't Drax just told her that he loved her and wanted to marry her?

'I don't want to leave you, but I'd better go and find Vere.'

'To tell him about us? Me?' Why was she asking that? Did she feel some kind of need to test Drax?

'To tell him about you, yes,' Drax agreed. After all, it was the truth.

CHAPTER TEN

'VERE! I didn't realise you were back until Sadie told me she'd seen you. I wasn't expecting you until tomorrow.'

Drax embraced his twin warmly. Vere would be amused when he told him that he had taken his advice and that he was going to marry Sadie himself, Drax admitted. Not that he intended to tell him yet. For the first time in his life Drax was experiencing an emotional need to separate himself slightly from his twin and keep the discovery of his love for Sadie within the special circle of intimacy that belonged to those newly in love. Yes, part of him wanted to tell not just Vere but the whole kingdom how he felt—that he had found the woman with whom he wanted to send the rest of his life—but another part of him wanted to hold Sadie close while they got used to the sensation of the world rocking slightly beneath their feet, reaching for mutual support at the awesome mystery of loving and being loved. The truth was that a part of him was so jealously protective of Sadie and their love that at the moment he didn't want to share its existence with anyone other than Sadie herself.

Because he wasn't entirely sure of that love? *No.* He was sure beyond any kind of doubt about his own feelings. But not Sadie's? Sadie loved him. He knew that.

'Drax, I was just about to come and find you. I want to talk to you about Sadie, and to offer you my apologies for not listening to you when you first spoke of her to me. She is charming. Quite irresistible. Delightfully so,' Vere emphasised softly, with a gleam in his eyes that turned Drax's stomach and filled him with an unfamiliar and furious jealousy.

Vere found Sadie attractive? He *wanted* her? He hadn't let himself think that this might happen, that Vere might want Sadie. But why not? Why shouldn't Vere recognise how wonderful she was, just as he had done?

'A beautiful young woman,' Vere continued approvingly. 'You were right to bring her to Dhurahn, and I was wrong. She is indeed perfect wife material.'

Vere was smiling expectantly at him, but the last thing Drax felt like doing was smiling. *Murderous* probably came closer to describing his feelings, he admitted bitterly. But he couldn't blame his twin for recognising, now that he had spoken with Sadie, just how lovable and wonderful she was, and acting to stake a claim on her. After all, *he* had been the one who had been stupid enough to suggest that Vere should marry her. And he was the one who had refused to accept his own reaction to her within minutes of having blackmailed her into getting into his car. He should have acted then, instead of being too proud to admit that he had fallen head over heels in love with her. He should have told Vere then. Not that he had found the perfect temporary wife for him, but that he had found the perfect, the only, permanent love for *himself*.

'Drax?'

He could hear the concern in his brother's voice, as well as see it in his eyes.

'What's wrong?'

'Nothing,' Drax said shortly. 'As you say, she will make a perfect wife.'

'You don't look very pleased that I'm agreeing with you. I expected you to be more enthusiastic than this,' Vere told him lightly.

Was there a subtle warning in Vere's words? A hint, perhaps, that he was on the verge of guessing his feelings? A reminder that Vere, as the elder twin, had the right to 'first choice'? Drax could taste the acid bitterness of his own jealousy. He could feel its burning heat and its savaging pain. He had never imagined he could harbour such feelings toward his twin, nor had he imagined that there would come a day when his love for a woman would be so intense and so total that she and it would eclipse the bond he had with Vere.

But he was, Drax reminded himself, a man of principle. It wasn't, after all, Vere's fault that he too had fallen for Sadie. They shared the same genes, so why shouldn't they love the same woman? But only one of them could have her. And he had already promised her to Vere.

Why didn't he tell his twin that he had changed his mind? That he had already declared his feelings to Sadie and that she, in turn, returned them? an inner voice urged him. He was tempted to listen to it and take its advice—but how could he? He was a man of honour, a man of his word, and he had already given Vere a promise that he should have

Sadie. How could he tell him that he had changed his mind and now wanted her for himself? How could he force his twin to suffer the dark bitterness of the emotions now gripping him?

So he was prepared to sacrifice his love for his twin, and he was prepared to sacrifice Sadie as well, was he? After she had told him she loved him? Was that fair to her? No, Sadie might believe she loved him, but Vere was more worthy of her love, Drax decided bleakly. Vere's were the shoulders that carried the greater burden of responsibility for their country. How could he, his twin, who knew him better than anyone else, see him denied the love and companionship of a woman as unique as Sadie? And she would learn to love Vere. How could she not do so? She would love him, and bear his children, and in time he—

The savagery of the pain that gripped him almost made him cry out. These were thoughts of a future he could not and would not endure. Sadie was *his*! Less than an hour ago he had only just stopped himself from making her his. If he hadn't done so, right now within her there could have been the life force that would create their child...

The darkest of thoughts stormed through his mind, both tempting and threatening his loyalty to his twin. The Drax who was so deeply in love with Sadie wanted to destroy anything and anyone who might come between them and take her from him. But the Drax who was Vere's twin fought against the dark pull of those feelings.

As he struggled to overcome them, Vere watched his twin with a small frown. Drax's reaction wasn't what he had been expecting.

'Drax, if there's a problem you want to discuss with me...?' he began.

This was Drax's opportunity to confide in his twin, to ask him to step back and allow him to claim Sadie, but a mixture of loyalty and pride refused to let him do so. Even if Vere agreed that he should have Sadie, how could he ever be sure that Vere might not regret his decision and...and what? Blame him for taking Sadie from him? Try to steal her away from him? How could he ever feel the same way about his twin? How could there be that bond of absolute trust and loyalty between them there had always been? How could he trust himself not to betray it? Drax wondered bitterly. And yet that knowledge couldn't make him regret what he and Sadie had already shared. He would carry the memory of that sweetness locked away within himself until his dying day.

'No, there isn't a problem. Why should there be?' he asked Vere flatly.

Drax was withholding something from him, Vere sensed, but his pride would not allow him to press the point and insist on an explanation. They were grown men now, after all, not children and each was entitled to his privacy.

As always when he was hurt Vere retreated into the austere aloofness that Drax normally coaxed him out of.

For once Drax was too caught up in his own feelings to notice Vere's deliberate emotional withdrawal from him.

'The Minister of State wishes to remind us that it is the anniversary of the creation of our country as an independent state next week.' Vere's clipped voice broke the heavy tension of their shared silence. 'He has made arrangements for the normal celebratory visit to the Oasis of the Two Doves. I take it you will be going?'

'Yes.' Drax's voice was as terse as Vere's.

'And Sadie will also be attending, I hope?'

Just hearing his twin say Sadie's name was like having a knife twisted in his gut.

'If that is your wish,' Drax replied woodenly.

'Given the circumstances, it certainly seems appropriate to me that she should be there,' Vere told him quietly. Couldn't Drax see how much he was hurting him by shutting him out like this? Or was it that he simply didn't care? Vere had never felt more isolated and alone. 'Indeed, I don't think it merely appropriate, I consider it very necessary that she should be a recognised part of the Royal party,' he added.

'If you say so,' Drax agreed curtly.

'I do.'

They were almost on the verge of falling out—and over a woman. Not just *a* woman, Drax told himself, but *the* woman…*his* woman. The woman he must now give up. How was he going to bear it? And Sadie? What of her feelings? She had, after all, given *him* her love. She was sexually innocent, yearning to be loved and to give her love in return. If she could love him after the way he had initially behaved towards her then surely she could and would love Vere? Would she close her eyes in

Vere's bed and think of him? The torturous images that sprang to life fully formed inside his head shocked him. He must not allow them to take root there. He must put Vere first. He *must!*

Sadie looked uncertainly towards Drax. It hadn't been until the early hours of the morning that she had finally given up hoping that he would come to her and had gone to bed. As a consequence, even though it was now mid-morning, she was heavy-eyed with lack of sleep and the weight of a growing certainty that something was wrong.

For a start, Drax was ignoring all her desperate attempts to make eye contact with him. For another thing, the only contact of any kind she had had with him since he had told her he loved her had been the arrival of the maid this morning to tell her that she was to be formally presented to Vere and that she should dress accordingly. Nothing else. Not a word nor a gesture. Nothing.

She couldn't remember a time when she had felt more emotionally insecure and abandoned, Sadie admitted. She actually felt worse than she had done when her parents had divorced. In the space of a few hours she had gone from feeling so high on happiness and love that she couldn't imagine her life being any more perfect, to feeling so insecure and anxious that it was hard for her to believe that Drax had actually told her he loved her. Even worse, she was beginning to find it all too easy to imagine that Drax, having almost taken her to bed, was now regretting whatever it was that had driven him to desire her. If he *did* love her, as he had claimed, then as far as she was concerned there was no way he wouldn't have made at least some effort to make sure that she knew he meant what he had said. If he *did* love her then surely he would want to let her know how much he longed to be with her instead of virtually ignoring her?

Was he behaving like this because he was afraid that his twin might not approve of their relationship? Sadie frowned. She didn't want to think of the man she loved being someone who needed to have the approval of someone else to validate his love. However, she was trying to be logical, and to accept that Drax and Vere were twins and that twins had a special relationship. Which was why she was here right now, wearing the cream suit Drax had told her he wanted her to wear for her first meeting with his brother. She looked longingly towards Drax, but he still wasn't looking at her. Deliberately?

His twin, on the other hand, was most certainly looking at her. Studying her silently, his expression withdrawn and austere.

Being treated like this by Drax wasn't just humiliating, it was also unbearably painful. When he had left her the previous day she had been on an emotional and sexual high. Then it had been easy to believe that he had meant what he'd said—that he did indeed love her. After all, she loved him. She had even got as far as wondering about names for their first baby before she had begun to feel the chill wind of her own anxiety. Then she had sat in her room, counting the minutes, aching to see Drax and to be reassured that she had not simply imagined what had happened between them. But Drax hadn't appeared. And so eventually she had gone to sleep, hugging to herself the memory of the precious time they had shared instead of hugging Drax.

Now, of course, it was abundantly plain to her what that happened. Drax had got carried away by sexual desire and had said things to her that he had later regretted. The distance he was deliberately creating between them now was his way of making sure that she realised how he felt—or rather how he didn't feel. Mingling with her pain was anger. Was he keeping his back towards her because he was afraid that if he looked at her she would behave like a complete fool and fling herself into his arms, begging him to tell her he loved her? Well, she might *feel* like doing that, but she had some pride. Certainly enough to make it plain to him that he had nothing to fear from her.

Determinedly Sadie kept her own back towards him as she answered the questions Vere was asking her. He was so different from Drax. Being with him, looking at him, listening to him and talking with him, did not cause her heart to pound with the force of the love-induced adrenalin surging through her veins. There was no sense of breathless awareness, no stomach-clenching tension, no fevered and tormented longing to rip off Vere's clothes and greedily satisfy her need to possess him. Vere was just a very pleasant man, with a kind smile, who looked like the man she loved. There was no chemistry between them—nothing other than a curiosity about him because he was Drax's twin.

She already knew without having to turn round that Drax had moved and was standing closer to her. She could feel the heat coming off her body and she yearned to step back into him, to turn around so that she could touch him, kiss him. The pain of not being able to was so savage that it contorted her body and stopped her breath.

Drax took a step towards Sadie. She wasn't looking at him. She was too busy smiling at Vere. He knew that she *had* looked at him when she had been escorted into the Presence Chamber, but he had not allowed himself to look back at her, knowing that if he did so he would not be able to stop himself from claiming her. He couldn't bear to give her up, but at the same time he couldn't allow himself to break his vow to give his first and total loyalty to his twin. The fault was his own. If he had not made that boast to Vere that he would find him a wife, if he had not offered Sadie to Vere… But he *had* done those things, and it was not Vere's fault that he too had recognised how special she was. Just listening to the soft warmth in her voice as she answered Vere's questions filled Drax with such a surge of murderous jealousy that when it subsided he felt physically sick with self-disgust. He loved her. How could he endure not just a future without her but seeing her happy with his twin?

CHAPTER ELEVEN

'SO THIS oasis is where the agreement was signed?' Sadie was forcing herself to smile and appear light-hearted as she waited for Vere to answer her.

It had been Hakeem who had come to her, two days after Drax had told her he loved her and then turned his back on her, to tell her excitedly that she was to join the Royal party at the traditional annual celebration to mark the original signing of the agreement when Dhurahn had become part of the newly formed union of independent Arab states at the Oasis of the Two Doves, on the edge of the desert's empty quarter.

They had arrived at the oasis late the previous afternoon to find a small but very luxurious encampment of traditional black pavilions erected close to the oasis, and smiling staff on hand to attend to their every need.

Once inside the large pavilion assigned to her, Sadie had been awed by its luxury and comfort. She even had her own private bathroom, complete with a shower.

But what she didn't have was Drax. The oasis was beautiful, but her misery was making it impossible for her to enjoy and appreciate it. She hadn't been able to eat the breakfast she had been served, and she had come here, to this quiet part of the oasis away from the tents, to hide her confusion and misery from everyone else and to try to decide what she should do.

And now here was Vere, who had been so charming to her, and so kind, but who just wasn't the man she wanted and loved. While Drax, whom she did love and want, was behaving as though she did not exist. No wonder she felt so sick at heart.

'Has Drax told you that we are having to cut short our stay at the oasis?' Vere asked.

Sadie shook her head, unable to bring herself to admit that Drax hadn't said a word to her since they had arrived the previous evening.

'We have received a warning that a sandstorm is veering this way, far more severe than first expected, so regrettably we cannot remain.'

'The oasis is lovely,' Sadie told him listlessly. She had seen how much Vere loved the desert, and his own obvious disappointment made her feel that she should offer some kind of sympathetic response.

'Indeed—but the desert can be fatally cruel to those who treat her lightly. Did you enjoy last night's ceremony?' he asked her.

'Yes. It's a heartwarming tradition.' Sadie tried to sound enthusiastic.

'We certainly think so,' Vere replied. 'Our family had always ruled Dhurahn, of course, but we celebrate the signing of the agreement because it signifies Dhurahn's new era of peace between what were previously warring warrior tribes. When the agreement was signed, two doves were released as a symbol of peace and hope for the future. Drax and I have always celebrated the occasion at the oasis. As boys, it was something we looked forward to. To those born of the desert there is always that sense of homecoming and completion about living as our forebears did, in harmony with the desert, respecting its power over us. 'You look unhappy,' he added suddenly, in a quieter tone, catching Sadie off guard.

She could feel her emotions tightening her throat. She bowed her head, not wanting to shame herself by letting Vere see her tears. But to her surprise Vere leaned forward and took hold of her hand, raising it to his lips. His kiss was kind, but meaningless to her, Sadie admitted wearily. Just as every man's kiss would be to her from now on. Because he wouldn't be Drax.

Vere watched Sadie in silence. He could see how upset she was, and he didn't want to upset her further. A little to his own surprise, Vere had discovered that the more he got to know Sadie, the deeper his feelings with regard to her had become. She would make a perfect royal consort as far as he was concerned. But now it seemed, from his behaviour towards her, that Drax no longer shared that view. It was, he decided, time that he spoke to Drax and found out exactly what was going on. He had held off questioning his twin directly in the hope that

Drax would come to him and speak openly, and it saddened and hurt him that Drax hadn't done so.

Drax frowned as he watched Vere and Sadie. He could feel the now-familiar sensation of unbearable emotional agony ripping into him. He wanted to go to them and physically push his twin aside, then take hold of Sadie so that Vere couldn't touch her. He knew that Sadie herself didn't understand what was happening. He could see it in her eyes. But how could he explain to her that Vere was claiming her?

Vere had just left her when some instinct made Sadie turn her head just in time to see Drax disappearing inside his pavilion. Her heart felt as though it was being torn apart. She couldn't endure any more of this torture. She had to know the truth; she had to know if Drax had ever loved her or if he had simply been cold-bloodedly lying to her. And if so, why? Not because he had hoped to trick her into his bed, obviously! She would go and have it out with him now, before she lost her courage, she decided. And she would demand that he return her passport to her so that she could leave Dhurahn. Her mind made up, Sadie made her way back through the busy bustle of men working to break up the camp and prepare for their return journey.

Already the hot bright glare of the sun had become slightly dimmed, the sky taking on an ominous, sulphurous tinge. But it was the storm inside herself that concerned Sadie more than the sandstorm threatening the oasis as she headed for the black tent she knew to be Drax's.

The tents had already been erected when they'd arrived, and Sadie had been bemused to discover just how luxurious the drab black structures crouched on the sand were on the inside. Her own was carpeted with beautiful Persian rugs and divided into a bedroom and a sitting area, both of which were furnished with luxurious fabrics, rich silks and velvets strewn over low divans, and a wide, lonely bed in which she had been unable to sleep because of her longing for Drax. She had tortured herself with imagining Drax in his own bed. How she had longed to be sharing the scented darkness of his pavilion and its privacy with Drax. In her mind's eye she had seen herself going to him, as secretly as though she were a favoured slave girl summoned to her master, crouching at the foot of his bed, waiting his permission to slowly caress and kiss her way up his naked body. But Drax did not want her kisses. He did not want *her*. He had made that plain enough.

A group of men were working outside Drax's pavilion, causing Sadie to hesitate, wary of just walking inside in full view of them, knowing the strict moral conventions Vere and Drax's subjects followed. There was another, smaller side entrance, though, just as there was in her own tent, and she headed for that

Drax was working on his computer when Vere walked into his tent. He frowned, pushing back his chair and standing up.

'The storm is getting worse,' Vere told him.

Drax watched him grimly. Vere hadn't come here to tell him that.

'I want to talk to you about Sadie,' Vere said quietly. 'You're in love with her, aren't you?'

Drax couldn't make himself deny it. 'What if I am? It doesn't affect you.'

'Of course it does. We've always shared everything, Drax.'

Sadie had managed to slip unnoticed into Drax's tent, but now, as she heard the two brothers' voices, she panicked and turned to leave. When she tried she discovered that the exit had been blocked by the men working outside, their four-wheel drive now parked close by. What on earth was she to do? She couldn't leave, but she certainly couldn't brazenly walk in on the two brothers either. She would just have to stay here until either Vere or both of them left.

She heard Vere saying something, but as always it was Drax's voice her senses registered more clearly, clinging to it with all the desperation of the lover who was unloved. She was pathetic, she derided herself. But the sound of her own name had Sadie stiffening and creeping closer to the fabric wall separating her from the brothers.

'So we share her, do we? How? In bed?' Drax could hear the emotion he couldn't control cracking his voice. 'Turn and turn about? Until she's so dizzy she can't tell the difference between us?'

Sadie went icy cold with shock, and then hot with fear. Nausea cramped her stomach and rose sourly in her throat.

In the semi-light of the richly furnished tent, Vere waited to let the bitterness and anger spew out of his twin before he spoke. But Sadie could not wait. Driven by revulsion and horror, she stumbled back towards the narrow exit she had used to enter the tent and pushed her way through the workmen, no longer caring how it would look.

She was out of hearing range when Vere stepped towards Drax and placed his hands on his shoulders, ignoring Drax's attempts to push him off. 'Why are you saying these things?' he asked him. 'I like Sadie, yes. But I do not desire her. When I think of her, I think of her as the woman you love.'

Outside, the wind had picked up dramatically, making Sadie stagger as she felt its full force. They would soon be returning to the city, but she couldn't wait that long for her escape or for oblivion.

A Land Rover had pulled up almost in front of her, its driver getting out and leaving the engine running as he hurried to help two other men who were staggering under the weight of what they were carrying. Without giving herself time to rationalise what she was doing, Sadie ran to it, ignoring the grains of sand tearing at her exposed skin and burning her eyes and mouth as she climbed into the vehicle and pulled the door closed after her. In front of her was a barely discernible track. She released the brake and put her foot on the accelerator.

Immediately the powerful off-roader surged forward into the seething storm. Sadie didn't care that she might be putting herself in danger. What was physical danger to her now, after what she had just heard? Her heart lurched against her ribs. She had thought that the worst pain she would ever have to bear was knowing that Drax didn't love her. But she had been wrong and naïve. So stupidly naïve. How many other women had been used by Drax and his brother as they had planned to use her? She knew there were those who might boast that they would enjoy such an experience, but she was not one of them. The thought of the two men touching her intimately, using her body for their pleasure, excited by the knowledge that they were sharing her, filled her with disgust and loathing.

Vere held Drax's bitter gaze as he waited for his twin to respond. The silence seemed to go on for ever, but finally Drax exhaled and said thickly, 'Vere, you are just saying that for my sake, because you know that I love her too. But you forget that you have already told me that she will make a perfect wife.'

'Yes,' Vere agreed. 'But for *you,* not for me. I had hoped my words would encourage you to confide in me and confirm what I had already guessed—that despite the fact that you had insisted you were bringing Sadie to Dhurahn for me you had fallen in love with her yourself. Do you really think I am so blind, so insensitive to your feelings, that I wouldn't know immediately how you felt about her? Although I have to say, after the way you have been treating her these last few days, I wouldn't blame Sadie for doubting how you feel about her. You've practically ignored her, and—'

'I did that for *your* sake! Because I thought that you too had fallen in love with her.'

'And it was for *your* sake that I didn't ask what was going on.' There was a hint of self-reproach as well as compassion in Vere's voice. 'I should have spoken more openly to you. But you know that I am not as comfortable in my emotional skin as you are in yours. I told myself that were I in your shoes I would want to choose the moment to tell you of my feelings rather than have you confront me with them. I knew something was wrong, but I had no idea what you were thinking. I should have guessed.'

'How could you?' Drax told him, sensing that this twin was blaming himself for what that happened. 'It is a well-known fact that when a man falls passionately and deeply in love he is lost to all reason. I assumed that because I love Sadie you must do the same. I was jealous, bitterly so, but I felt I had to stick to my statement to you that I was bringing Sadie back to Dhurahn for *you.*'

'Have you told Sadie any of this?'

'No. I couldn't bring myself to do so.'

'She is very distressed by your behaviour towards her,' Vere told him gently.

'She told you that?'

Now Vere could smile, as he heard and recognised the reason for the hostility in his twin's voice. 'Not as such. But it is plain to me that she is unhappy.'

While they had been speaking the noise of the wind had been increasing, to the point where now they had to talk loudly to make themselves heard above it.

'We need to return to the city,' Vere said. 'We don't want to be caught out here in the storm.'

'I'll drive Sadie back myself,' Drax said. 'And the first thing I shall want to do when we get back is set in hand the arrangements for my marriage—after I have apologised to her.'

Suddenly they were both laughing, embracing one another with genuine understanding and mutual happiness.

As they stepped back, one of the workmen suddenly burst into the tent, exclaiming, 'Highness! The English girl has just driven out of the camp in one of the Land Rovers.'

Drax released Vere and turned to look at the anxious man who had come hurrying into the tent.

'What?'

It couldn't be possible that Sadie had done something so dangerous. But the look on the workman's face confirmed that it was.

The two brothers ran for the exit.

Outside, men were battling against the strong winds to pack everything up, some of them bent almost double against the force. A thick veil of storm-driven sand was turning the landscape into a yellow fog.

'Which way did she go?' Drax yelled at the workman above the keening howl of the wind.

The man pointed in the direction of the eye of the storm. Drax and Vere exchanged grim looks.

'I'm going after her,' Drax said.

'You can't—you won't—' Vere began, and then stopped when he saw the expression in his twin's eyes. 'I'm coming with you,' he said instead.

Drax shook his head, but the look he gave his twin was filled with love and gratitude.

'No, Vere,' he told him gruffly. 'We both know that I *have* to go after her, even though we also know the danger. My life is nothing without her.'

'As is mine without you, my brother,' Vere said simply.

Tears burned the backs of Drax's eyes. 'You will go on because you must—because our people and our country need you. But I cannot go on without Sadie. Before I met her I would have sworn that there could be no bond, no love that could ever be as strong as what I share with you. But Sadie has shown me that I was wrong. I have to find her.'

'And if you don't?'

'I won't rest until I do. I won't come back until I find her. And I *will* find her. Even if I have to search the desert through this life and eternity for her.'

Vere gave a small nod of his head.

'Go, then, my brother,' he said softly. 'And my prayers go with you. We will leave the generator and one of the tents, just in case you should need it.'

Drax nodded his own head. They embraced again, and Vere stood and watched as Drax ducked under the ferocity of the wind and climbed into his four-wheel drive.

'Excellency, we must leave soon,' one of the workmen begged Vere urgently.

Vere nodded, but didn't move until the whirling sand had swallowed up Drax's vehicle and he could see him no longer.

Outside the windows the sand whirled and the wind howled, battering the vehicle from all directions. Sadie had long ago lost sight of the track she had been following, but she didn't care. She didn't care about anything. She only wanted oblivion.

A sob tore at her throat, her emotions shaking her body in much the same way as the storm shook the vehicle. Both she and the vehicle were in the grip of a force so powerful that they could not escape from it. The storm was threatening to pluck up the heavy car and mercilessly destroy it, but it wasn't that that was making the dry sobs tear at Sadie's throat. Drax! How could he have planned to subject her to such degradation? She couldn't bear to think of the fate he had been willing to inflict on her, and she couldn't bear to know that she had loved him. She wanted to tear his memory from her heart and her mind.

The vehicle's engine started to race as it

struggled to climb a steep, invisible incline—so steep that it must almost be perpendicular, Sadie realised, as the wheels spun and the vehicle rocked. Without warning it suddenly started to plunge downwards at great speed.

Sadie tried to brake, but it was no use. The vehicle was out of control. She cried out in the seconds before the vehicle lurched to an abrupt halt, causing her to bang her head on the window, and through the pain she was aware that she had cried out Drax's name. And the pain of knowing *that* was far greater than the injury to her throbbing head. Her forehead felt wet and sticky. She lifted her hand to it and saw that she was bleeding. Already she could barely see through the windscreen because of the sand. She knew she ought to be afraid, but somehow she wasn't. What was the point? Right now dying felt easier than living with the knowledge of Drax's cruelty.

Sadie couldn't have got very far, Drax tried to reassure himself. She had driven off down a well-used track, according to the driver of the off-roader she had taken. But she had also driven right into the path of the oncoming storm—which was why he had refused Vere's offer to come with him.

That he would find Sadie was not in doubt. Whether they would survive the fury of the storm was a different matter. Like all modern vehicles in use in Dhurahn for desert travel, both were fitted with a special tracking system that ensured a driver could not become lost in the desert. His mobile phone might not work in the ferocity of the storm, but the tracking device would. Which was just as well, Drax thought, well aware of how easily a sandstorm could change the landscape, wiping out its existing features and creating new ones. It was impossible for him to see very much through his windscreen, but unlike Sadie he knew exactly what to do when he suddenly started to climb a steep sandhill.

Even though he knew approximately where the other vehicle was, it still took Drax several precious minutes to locate it, half buried beneath the sand. When he wrenched open the door and saw Sadie slumped over the driving wheel he felt as though his heart was being forcibly ripped out of his chest. But the moment he touched her she jerked upward, her eyes opening and darkening with horror as she saw him.

'No! Not you… No…' She was crying and half hysterical as she tried to push him away, to stop him from lifting her out of the car, but Drax persevered, dragging her free as she collapsed against him. Bent almost double under her weight, he struggled back to his own vehicle. Already sand was drifting against it, driven there by the unrelenting wind. Drax knew there was no chance of them making it back to Dhurahn ahead of the storm, but if they stayed here it would overwhelm them. The oasis was their best chance of survival— if they could get there.

Somehow he managed to manhandle Sadie into the passenger seat. He had left the engine running, and as he put the vehicle in gear Sadie started to come round.

She was with Drax. Sadie shuddered. Why had he come after her? Why hadn't he just left her in peace? Was he so perverted that he would risk death rather than be denied his sick pleasure?

Tears filled her eyes and spilled down on her cheeks.

Drax reached out his hand to touch her, and immediately she cowered away from him, her eyes bleak with pain.

'What are you doing here? Why did you come after me?'

'Because I had no choice. I love you, Sadie. You are my life and—'

'No.' How dared he lie to her like this when she knew the truth? How dared he look at her with a pain in his gaze that said she was more precious to him than life itself?

She started to laugh, almost hysterically.

'Yes!' he insisted. But Sadie shook her head.

'You're lying. You don't love me. I heard you, Drax; I heard everything you said about me to Vere. About the two of you sharing me.' She made herself say the horrible words and endure the poison of their taste. 'I won't let you do that to me, Drax. I'd rather die,' she said wildly. 'I won't let you abuse me like that.'

'Was that why you left the camp?' Drax demanded.

'You didn't think I'd stay, did you, after hearing something like that?'

Sadie gasped as the wind howled and

screamed, buffeting the four-wheel drive and causing it to rock from side to side.

'Sadie, it isn't as it seems.'

'How can it *not* be? I heard you.'

'I know you did, but…' Drax cursed under his breath as he fought to control the vehicle. 'I love you, Sadie.'

'Don't say that! You're lying.'

'No, I'm not. What you heard me saying to Vere was—'

His explanations would have to wait until they got back to the oasis, Drax realised, as the wind died abruptly and suddenly there was complete silence.

'What—?' Sadie began uncertainly, sensing that the unnatural calm had a dangerous malevolence about it.

'The eye of the storm,' Drax told her grimly. 'If we're lucky, very lucky, we might make it to the oasis before all hell breaks loose. There it is up ahead—see?'

Sadie could. The camp had an abandoned, empty air about it; several of the palm trees had been uprooted, one of them having crashed down into the oasis itself. Drax brought the vehicle to a halt alongside the one remaining tent—Drax's tent, Sadie saw.

'Where are the others? Vere?' Sadie asked, almost stammering over his twin's name as she remembered what she had heard him saying.

'Back in Dhurahn by now. You drove straight into the path of the storm. Quick,' he commanded her, unbuckling his seatbelt and turning to unfasten hers. Sadie shook her head. She wanted to refuse to get out of the Land Rover, but the eerie silence was somehow more frightening than the thought of being with him. At least she knew that only he was here.

She wouldn't let him touch her, though, not even as she struggled through a deep drift of sand to cross the few feet that separated the vehicle from the entrance to the tent.

'We are lucky that the generator is still working,' Drax said once they were both inside. 'At least for now.'

'Maybe the storm is over and we don't need to stay here? Maybe we should try to get back to the city?' Sadie suggested. 'And when we do get there I want my passport back, Drax. I won't stay and be...abused.' She lifted her chin and said fiercely, 'If you and Vere want to play those sort of perverted games then you will have to find someone else to play them with.' Her face was burring with shame and disgust.

'Sadie—' Drax groaned, but he stopped speaking abruptly as suddenly, out of no-where, the silence was torn apart by an un-earthly sound as the wind returned to howl and scream its fury whilst tearing at the fabric of the pavilion as though it were an alien life force.

It was impossible to speak above its fury, but Sadie could see from Drax's expression the danger they were in. 'We're going to die, aren't we?' she whispered.

Drax must have read her lips, because he shook his head and mouthed back, 'If we do it will be together. And I would rather die with you, Sadie, than live without you.'

What was he saying? He couldn't possibly mean those words. To her disbelief, she saw that he was coming towards her. She tried to evade him, but it was too late. His arms closed round her and his mouth came down on hers in a fierce, possessive kiss.

She shouldn't be letting this happen. But somehow she couldn't stop herself from lifting her own arms to hold him close. Perhaps it was the knowledge that they might not survive that was fanning the embers of her need into such an urgent heat, making her return his kiss with equal hunger, urging her to take what there was before the darkness came down on them.

Outside the wind shrieked, but all Sadie could hear was the frantic thud of her own heartbeat and the voice inside her that said nothing mattered but this need within her. Her body ached and yearned for Drax's touch—and not just his touch, but his possession. She could feel her flesh heating, seeking a complete union with his, wanting at its most intimate level to draw him in and keep him there, to make him so much a part of her that there were no boundaries left between them and they were one perfect whole. This was all that mattered; it was all that she wanted to communicate to Drax.

She pressed her body up against his, willing him to respond to her need, to answer her impatient hunger, to have him destroy the barriers between them, to answer the storm inside her and tear away everything that separated them so that they could be truly together, flesh on flesh, heart on heart, until she possessed him deep within her.

Somewhere a small part of her registered that she was being driven by a form of madness, but her need scorned it. What was madness but a delicious form of intense reality? And nothing could be more real than this. She could feel Drax's hands moving urgently over her body. She moaned with hot, hungry pleasure, sliding her own hand down his back and then over the curve of his buttock, and then between their bodies so that she could touch him intimately. She felt him shudder when her flingers closed over him, and she shuddered herself in response, lost mindlessly in the storm of her need for him.

'Take me to bed, Drax,' she begged fiercely. 'Here and now, when it's just the two of us. I want you so much…'

'No.' His denial was low and raw, the aching, tormented sound of a man refusing what he wanted most. 'No, Sadie,' he repeated, releasing her. 'Not until I have talked with you. Explained everything to you.'

'We might not live that long,' Sadie said. 'And if we don't, I want my last moments with you to be in your arms, Drax. Not—'

Drax gave her a small shake. You mustn't say that. We are going to live. Now, let me explain—'

'Not here.' Sadie was being driven by an instinct she didn't understand but could no longer fight. 'Tell me in bed, Drax, while you're holding me.' What she meant was that a part of her didn't want to see his face because she didn't want to see that he was lying to her.

'Very well,' Drax agreed. 'In bed, in my arms, you shall hear the truth and know my heart, Sadie.'

CHAPTER TWELVE

THEY undressed quickly, feverishly almost, aware not only of their intense desire for one another and the unresolved issues between them, but also of the threat of the storm and its power to destroy them. The fine grains of sand brushed easily from Sadie's skin as she stood staring at Drax's naked body, unable to stop greedily absorbing the sight of him. She could feel the fine tremble of his hands when he reached for her, holding her so tightly in his arms that she could feel the rapid beating of his heart as though it were her own. She wanted him so badly, and to judge from his state of arousal his need matched hers. Would he think about his twin later, when he possessed her? Would he imagine that Vere was with them? Would he—?

He touched her face gently and kissed her

forehead. 'Don't look like that, Sadie. What you overheard wasn't what you thought, although I can understand how damning it would sound.'

'You can't magic away the words you spoke, Drax.'

'No, I can't. But I can explain where they came from. The truth is that I spoke those words out of blind, driving jealousy and bitterness, Sadie. All our lives Vere and I have put our loyalty to one another and our relationship first. When I fell in love with you I discovered for the first time what it meant to hate my brother, to feel murderously jealous of him.'

'Why should you feel like that? You *knew* how I felt about you.'

'Yes, but the situation is more complicated that that. You see, I had promised you to Vere.' Drax felt her stiffen and try to pull away from him. But he had anticipated her reaction and held her tightly, keeping her close to him.

'You mean that you acted as a pimp for your brother?' Sadie challenged him savagely.

'No. Let me explain.'

Quietly and openly Drax started to tell her about the potential problems that might have arisen from the desire of the rulers of their neighbouring states to tie them to their families via marriage.

Sadie winced when she heard Drax repeating his mocking comment about virginal women falling in love with sheikhs, but Drax laughed softly and said, 'What I hadn't bargained for was that this sheikh was going to be the one falling in love, and that he would be so overwhelmed by the experience that he'd try to pretend that it wasn't happening.

'Vere guessed the truth, though. My brother isn't like me. He is more reserved. He finds it less easy to talk of what he feels, even to me, and he guards his emotional privacy fiercely. So he waited for me to come forward and tell him of my feelings. He tried to encourage me by commenting that you would make a perfect wife, and in my jealousy I imagined that he was telling me that he too had fallen in love with you and wanted you as his wife. How could he not love you when you're so loveable? How could I have so stupid as to not see that for myself the moment I set eyes on you?

'Because he is my twin, and because of the

vow I had made to find him a temporary wife first, I felt obliged to step out of your life. I had no idea that when he talked about you being perfect wife material he was referring not to himself but to me. It was the jealous outburst you overheard that enabled him to learn how I had misunderstood him. What you heard me saying to him was not, my darling, a description of what I wanted, but the anger of a bitterly jealous man. I hated the thought of Vere so much as looking at you, never mind touching you.'

'But you were still willing to give me up to Vere, even though you knew I loved you?'

'I reasoned that since Vere is the better of the two of us you would love him more. You have to understand, Sadie, that because of our obligations to our country Vere and I have always put our loyalty to one another ahead of everything else. But now both he and I know that our relationship can never be the same again, because my love for you means that *you* will now be the most important person in my life.'

Sadie could hear the sincerity and truth in his voice.

'I couldn't bear what I thought I'd heard you say. I'd wanted to talk to you. To tell you that I wanted to return to England.' She shuddered. 'I shouldn't have taken the vehicle like that, but I had to get away.'

'And I had to find you.'

'Oh, Drax, we could both die here, and it will be my fault.'

He shook his head and smiled at her. 'We aren't going to die. Listen.'

Sadie looked at him and frowned.

'I can't hear anything.'

'Exactly,' Drax said. 'While you and I were battling our own personal storm, the one outside the tent blew itself out.'

'We'll be able to leave here and return to Dhurahn?' Would he sense her disappointment and guess how reluctant she was to give up the chance of this precious time alone with him?

'We could,' he agreed. 'But not tonight.'

'Not tonight?' Sadie repeated.

'No, tonight.' Drax repeated firmly. 'Because tonight I want you to myself, so that I can prove to you just how much I love you.'

'I'd like that. And I'd like it too if our child was conceived here tonight, Drax,' Sadie told him softly. 'Here, tonight, in the aftermath of the storm which could have destroyed us.'

She could see from the smouldering look in his eyes just how much her words were affecting him. She leaned towards him, reaching out her hand to enclose him, trembling with anticipation and desire when her fingers encircled his hardness. His flesh felt hot, tempting her caress.

'You know what's going to happen if you keep on doing that, don't you?' Drax said thickly.

'Show me,' Sadie said, catching her breath as he lifted her hand from his body.

He kissed her fiercely as his own hands mapped *her* body. When his hands cupped her breasts her nipples rose eagerly, seeking the touch of his flesh. His lips were against her throat, feeling the vibration of her moans of delight at the soft tug of his fingers and thumbs on her nipples. Sadie lifted her hands to his shoulders, pushing his head further down her body, wanting the erotic stimulation of his mouth against her breast. But when he obeyed her unspoken command the pleasure was shockingly sharper than she had anticipated.

Drax slipped his hand between her legs as he drew her nipple into his mouth, the knowing stroke of his fingertip probing the folded outer lips of her sex mirroring the rhythmic tug of his mouth of her nipple.

Sadie thought she would die from the pleasure building so intensely inside her—or explode, its tension was so unbearably arousing. She opened her legs and pressed up against his hand, hotly eager for him to probe deeper and more intimately at the slickness of her aroused flesh. He had found the source of her female pleasure and was caressing it, drawing it to its full desire-swollen sensitivity, so that every shallow breath she took seemed to rock her on the edge of the orgasm she longed to engulf her. But each time she reached for it Drax withdrew from her, until she reached for him in a frenzy of need, telling him fiercely, 'Now, Drax. Now, please now.'

It was heaven to feel the weight of him against her, to spread her legs and then wrap them around him tightly, arching up against him. He thrust carefully into her, but his care frustrated her.

'Deeper, Drax, harder,' she begged him, her eyes darkening with feral pleasure when he

obeyed her and she felt her body accommodate the sensation of him within it. Experi-
mentally she tightened her muscles around
him, and heard him groan with pleasure.

'How can you know how to do that?' he
demanded in between kisses.

'How can I not?' Sadie whispered back
against his lips. 'When it's what I want to
do…when I want to feel you and hold you…
when I want…'

'This?' he suggested, thrusting rawly, rhyth-
mically, faster and deeper, while she clung to
him and gave herself up to the pleasure of his
possession. His rhythm was taking her, driving
her, towards the pinnacle that was now so en-
ticingly within reach.

'Drax…' she appealed.

He drove harder, filling her, making her
move urgently against him, and she stiffened
as the pleasure exploded inside her, surge after
surge of it, in waves of exquisite pulsing sensation as her body gripped and caressed his
and she felt the liquid warmth of him spilling
into her.

'Drax,' she whispered, lifting her hand to
touch his face.

He captured it, pressing his lips to the palm of her hand and then saying rawly, 'You are mine now. Mine for ever. My love and soon, I hope, my wife. You will marry me, won't you, Sadie?'

She was too overwhelmed by her own emotions to do anything more than nod her head and let him hold her close while her body still quivered with small aftershocks of pleasure.

'Shouldn't you let Vere know that the storm is over and that you are safe?' Sadie asked drowsily. 'He's bound to be worrying.'

'There's no mobile signal out here, but don't worry. Vere will know that we are safe.'

'Because he's your twin and he will sense it?' Sadie asked him

'Yes.'

'But that doesn't mean he'll know you've found me.'

She could hear the love in his voice when he told her softly, 'Yes, it does. Because I told him when I left that I didn't intend to return from the desert without you.'

They were married three weeks later—first in a civil ceremony, and then in the traditional manner of Dhurahn's people, handfasted to one another by the tying of a silk scarf around their wrists as Drax held Sadie's hand firmly in the grasp of his own, their fingers interlinked.

It was Vere who officiated at the ceremony, as Leader of his people, and Vere too who welcomed Sadie with the kindest of reassuring speeches—a public reiteration of the private assurance he had already given her that he was happy to welcome her as Drax's wife.

It was a long day, with feasting and traditional dancing and singing, but finally they were alone.

'I love you,' Drax whispered as he took her in his arms in the privacy of their own quarters.

Beyond the large window moonlight glinted on the pool from which she had seen him emerging naked and had wanted him so fiercely. She wanted him just as fiercely now. But now she was free to tell him so—and to show him. She looked up at him, her feelings illuminating her expression.

'When you look at me like that, I know that I am the most fortunate man on earth,' Drax told her softly. 'If I have one hope left now it is that Vere will find someone to love and be loved, as I love and am loved by you, Sadie.'

And then there was only silence, punctuated by the softness of Sadie's long sighs of pleasure as he celebrated with her their commitment to one another.

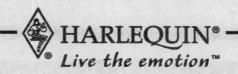

HARLEQUIN®
INTRIGUE®

BREATHTAKING ROMANTIC SUSPENSE

Shared dangers and passions lead to electrifying
romance and heart-stopping suspense!

Every month, you'll meet six new heroes
who are guaranteed to make your spine tingle
and your pulse pound. With them you'll enter
into the exciting world of Harlequin Intrigue—
where your life is on the line
and so is your heart!

THAT'S INTRIGUE—
ROMANTIC SUSPENSE
AT ITS BEST!

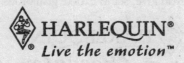

HARLEQUIN®
Live the emotion™

HARLEQUIN®
Presents

The world's bestselling romance series...
The series that brings you your favorite authors,
month after month:

Helen Bianchin...Emma Darcy
Lynne Graham...Penny Jordan
Miranda Lee...Sandra Marton
Anne Mather...Carole Mortimer
Susan Napier...Michelle Reid

and many more uniquely talented authors!

Wealthy, powerful, gorgeous men...
Women who have feelings just like your own...
The stories you love, set in exotic, glamorous locations...

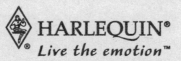